THE *Confection* CONNECTION

MONICA TILLERY

Author of *A Sweet Deal* and *Adam's Ambition*

CRIMSON ROMANCE

F+W Media, Inc.

Published by
Crimson Romance
an imprint of F+W Media, Inc.
10151 Carver Road, Suite 200
Blue Ash, OH 45242. U.S.A.
www.crimsonromance.com

ISBN 10: 1-4405-8870-8
ISBN 13: 978-1-4405-8870-9
eISBN 10: 1-4405-8871-6
eISBN 13: 978-1-4405-8871-6

Cover art © 123RF/Sven Bannuscher and Shutterstock/wavebreakmedia

*For Christine Grazioli, who always knows
when to show up with cake*

Chapter One

Carly Piper hung up the phone and blew out an aggravated breath. Last week, a refrigerator went out, costing her several hundred dollars she couldn't exactly spare, and now an oven? Her bakery, Caketopia, couldn't do without it, and with the biggest pitch of her life happening in less than an hour, she didn't have the time to deal with it. With a quick roll of her neck and shoulders, she mentally tallied the extra time it would take to handle the pitch without an assistant. Speaking of, her employee's heels clacked on the tile floor, announcing her imminent arrival. How Layla Jameson managed to work in those shoes confounded Carly.

"Hey, I was just about to find you. I've got a repair guy coming for the oven, so I need you to stay here. I'll have to go on the pitch alone." Carly untied her apron and hung it on a hook.

"Are you sure? That's a lot of stuff to carry." Layla towered over Carly, especially in those ridiculous shoes. "It'll be crowded, and you might have to make more than one trip. With nobody there to help you—"

"I don't see any way around it. If we don't get this stupid oven fixed, we'll fall behind on this week's orders. With my luck, the other one will probably go out, too."

Layla laughed, then stopped when she saw that Carly wasn't joking. Between the constant repairs, the economy, and competition, Caketopia struggled to remain successful. Getting this job could mean the beginning of a new era for Carly and her business. Sure, it would be easier to concentrate on the pitch if Layla went with her, but she was a professional. She could win over the celebrity couple planning their wedding without help. She had to.

"All right," Layla said. "I'll go load the van, at least. You just get ready, and I'll see you outside."

Carly packed her bag with binders that held photos of her work, Caketopia information she could leave with the couple, and a contract ready for them to sign if things went her way. After kicking off her rubber clogs, she slipped her feet into much less comfortable but infinitely more flattering shoes before swiping fresh gloss across her lips and heading out to the van. Hopefully the desperation would be replaced by her usual calm professionalism by the time she arrived at the swanky uptown hotel.

A blast of warm air greeted her as she crossed the parking lot to her refrigerated van. Layla, ever the mind-reader, had already turned the van on, ensuring that it would be nice and cool for the drive to the hotel. There, Carly would either secure the biggest job of her career, guaranteeing more business than she could dream of, or come back to the same old thing, paying bills she could scarcely afford. Before she second-guessed herself any more, Carly opened the door and slid in, noting with satisfaction that she could at least afford the new van. Now she didn't have to worry about snagging her clothes on the ragged vinyl of her old delivery vehicle. The smooth new seats and cold air conditioning reminded her of how far she'd already come.

She rolled down the window. "Wish me luck!" What she meant was more like, *Cross your fingers and toes because getting this job means we'll be set from now on*, but she gave Layla a bright smile.

"Knock 'em dead, boss," Layla said with a little wave as she squinted in the sunlight.

Carly pulled out of the parking lot and navigated the van through Dallas traffic to Central Expressway, and started to relax as the city flew past. She was an accomplished professional, an award winner in her field, and the chance to make the cakes for a high-profile celebrity wedding should feel exciting. It shouldn't feel like she was heading for the trial of her life. Being prepared always boosted her confidence, so she reviewed her spiel, which, after delivering it for so many years, she could recite in her sleep.

Now all she had to do was show up and wow the client. No problem, right?

Before long, she was dodging paparazzi and curious onlookers as she turned toward the back of the hotel. Celebrities visiting Dallas often stayed at the hot spot, and the news must be out that country music superstar Rusty Grainger and his notoriously quirky fiancée, actress Sequoia Rivers were on site. At the service entrance, Carly parked the van and got to work stacking her signature lavender bakery boxes into neat rows on a dolly. She hoisted her oversized canvas bag over her shoulder and trekked through the parking garage to the door. Once inside, Carly took in the hotel's lush, almost bacchanalian atmosphere with wide eyes and an appreciation for the stunning attention to detail. From the gleaming black marble floors to the plush burgundy brocade on the walls, the place screamed elegant debauchery. She parked the dolly and fished a card out of her pocket to check the suite name once more before the elevator arrived.

Ensconced in the tiny decadent space, she concentrated on her breathing, reminding herself that her work was top-notch. Best to focus on the positive and try to forget how badly she needed the business. As the elevator slowed, she adjusted her bag on her shoulder and held her head high. The doors whooshed open, and silence greeted her. Silence, a near empty hallway, and Michael Welch.

He whistled innocently as she rolled her eyes. Without so much as flinching under her withering gaze, he brushed past her into the elevator. "Going up, Carly?"

He tapped the "close door" button and stood an inch away from her. Of course *he* would be here. Why hadn't she anticipated that? She'd met Michael Welch three years ago when they were rival contestants on the Cuisine Network's popular reality competition show *Sugar Shock*, where hopeful bakers battled to create exciting cakes and pastries and complete ridiculous challenges. His charisma, charm, and talent—combined with thick brown hair, a chiseled jaw, and piercing green eyes—made it hard for Carly to reconcile her attraction to him with her irritation. Everyone—show personnel, other contestants, the viewers—seemed to love him, but everything he did rubbed Carly the wrong way. He was almost too good-looking and too personable.

For Carly, the two high points of the *Sugar Shock* experience came on the day she found out she'd been accepted for that season and the day she was voted off and could get away from Michael. Spending months with him on set hadn't endeared him to her, but he'd somehow managed to pull her under his magnetic spell. They'd shared a confusing and stupid kiss—moments before the challenge that sealed her fate, of course. No matter how much he protested and pleaded innocence, he knew what he was doing. She was thrown off her game and sent home, while he went on to compete in the final competition and won the whole thing. She wasn't even disappointed to be eliminated so close to the end, since it was such a relief to finally be rid of him.

Even though it was clear she wasn't cut out for cutthroat TV competitions, the experience and recognition that had come with the show brought new opportunities. Carly could finally open her own shop, where she happily spent her days creating beautiful confections to celebrate the most important days of her clients' lives. The work was invigorating and satisfying, everything she'd ever wanted.

They reached their floor, and Carly set her mind to ignore the memories evoked by his too-familiar cinnamon-chocolate scent.

"Nervous, cupcake?"

"Of course."

"Why? Because every hoity-toity bakery from here to Fort Worth is competing for the same job? Because you've suddenly decided that your cakes aren't fancy enough for primetime? Or is it because you finally get to see me again after all these years?"

He waggled his eyebrows suggestively, and the tension she'd been carrying around in her shoulders all day disappeared in a quick burst of laughter.

"Oh, yeah, that's it." She'd hoped for confident sarcasm, but heard a prim quality in her voice that made her cringe. Maybe breathing the same air would somehow help his confidence rub off on her. She ignored how warm her cheeks felt and gripped the handle of her bag.

"Come on. We got this." There was no "we," but she knew if she reminded him of that, he'd have a snappy comeback that would make her feel like a fool. He pulled his signature black skullcap tight over his head, his green eyes glinting with enthusiasm. Without asking, he commandeered her dolly and pulled it out of the elevator. "Let's roll."

"Didn't you bring samples or anything? Are you planning to win the couple over on charm alone?"

"I brought an assistant from my shop with me today, and she has my things. You happened to catch me on my way back upstairs from checking out the amenities. Don't worry about my pitch."

The view was just as good both coming and going, and she hated herself for noticing. Michael shot her one last look over his shoulder before heading down the hall, making her wonder if she'd broadcasted her thoughts.

Carly spent the short walk drawing from his confidence and trying to project some semblance of her own. Michael stopped outside the door, rapped twice, and stepped back. A wispy blonde dressed head to toe in black, holding a clipboard, and barking orders into a walkie-talkie answered.

"Names and business?" The blonde didn't look up as Carly and Michael each provided their information. "I have Michael Welch, and I have Caketopia. So which is it?"

"They're two separate businesses. Caketopia is mine, and The Clubhouse is his." Carly tried to see the listings on the page as the woman went through them again.

"Okay, well, we have one appointment left, and it's for Michael Welch of Caketopia. Who wants it?"

Carly's heart sank as she realized what had happened. She needed the job—her future nearly depended on it—but not if it meant pushing a legitimate competitor out of the way to get it. "We have two separate bakeries, so we both want it."

"You can both go in if you share the appointment. The rest of the day is booked."

Michael patted Carly on the shoulder. "Come on. We'll split the time and explain what happened when we get in there."

"Are you sure?"

"Yep. Let's do this. The worst that can happen is neither one of us gets the job. We've got to at least try."

Michael nodded to the blonde woman, and she spoke into her walkie-talkie about the change of plans.

Carly was immediately glad that she'd let Michael talk her into sharing the appointment. The air was charged with excitement and possibility. The huge entourage necessary to staff the venture swirled around a common spot in the middle of the room, rushing around, chattering into phones, and checking clipboards. One of the country's most famous couples sat at an elaborately carved wooden table, in absurdly oversized purple velvet chairs, as though they were holding court.

As Carly looked around, taking everything in and mentally rehearsing her spiel, Michael strode through the crowd and headed straight to Rusty's table. He was in his element, sure of his abilities and that he was right where he belonged. That confidence was half the reason he'd won the reality show. His creative and fearless designs explained the rest.

Rusty Grainger, the groom, stood, and his eyes lit up with recognition.

"You're Michael Welch," he exclaimed. His head swiveled from one to the other. "And you're Carly Piper, from that show! What was it called, babe?" He turned to his fiancée, who was decidedly less impressed. Not surprising, given her reputation. Sequoia Rivers was a hugely famous movie star known more for her quirky new age habits than for her glitzy roles. She appeared to delight in not caring what or who was hot, and she wasn't likely to be drawn in by Michael's swagger or impressed by pseudo-famous bakers.

"*Sugar Shock*." She stopped short of rolling her eyes.

"You're hired, man." Rusty thrust his hand out, and Michael grabbed it, shaking heartily as they voiced their mutual admiration for one another. A short blonde bearing a dolly stacked with Michael's signature red-and-black bakery boxes arrived and silently unloaded his materials.

"Not so fast, honey. Let's at least taste the cakes first. Plus, I don't know if I want some chocolate-jalapeño cake shaped like an armadillo or something at our wedding." Fortunately, Carly was prepared to show both her classic, traditional designs as well as a few she'd created to reflect Sequoia's earthy, natural sensibilities.

Carly went to work organizing her own samples and portfolios, bolstered by Sequoia's obvious lack of enthusiasm for Michael. Customers appreciated Carly's elegant style, her ability to put fresh twists on classic design, and her impeccable attention to detail. She wasn't flashy, and she definitely wasn't famous, but she had built a name for herself. A reputation built on exquisite quality, cake by cake.

She lined up plates with small hand-lettered placards that labeled each flavor. She gave Rusty and Sequoia each a fork, then set up a binder full of cake photos for each of them. Michael did the same with the wilder flavors from his own shop. Carly then launched into her pitch. Experience had taught her that a groom's enthusiasm means nothing if the bride isn't interested. The bride's opinion is what really matters, when it comes down to it.

"These are the most popular flavors at Caketopia, but I would be delighted to work with you if there's something you want that you don't see here." She waved her hand over samples of her classic white chocolate cake and watched as they tasted bites of coconut, lemon, and Italian crème cake. "Many brides can't or don't want to choose just one, so we can do the layers in different flavors. We can also create something beautiful by mixing and matching frosting flavors and choosing different fresh fruits to complement your choices."

"If you want something a little less run of the mill, try these." Michael pushed his Mexican chocolate, red velvet, gingerbread, and toasted almond samples forward. "The Clubhouse offers frostings that are a bit more unique as well. Let's see, we've got Kahlua, mocha, chocolate peanut butter, and hazelnut. I can do more traditional choices as well."

Rusty tried Michael's cakes, obviously savoring each bite as he made appreciative noises, and Sequoia looked as though she were ready to slap somebody. It looked as though she would turn them both down just to get Michael away from the table.

"Sequoia, what do you have in mind for your wedding cake?" Carly took a chance, hoping that Sequoia was like most brides and could be diverted when given the chance to wax poetic about her big day. She wasn't disappointed.

Sequoia's face took on the dreamy look Carly had seen on countless brides before her. "I want it to be elegant, but sweet, you know? I want it to be special, unique, and even glamorous. If people saw it and thought of a fairy tale, that would be perfect." Mentally shelving the quirky nature-inspired designs she'd prepared, Carly nodded. She'd expected to hear that Sequoia dreamt of an environmentally responsible wedding, maybe something spiritual or nature-inspired. An elegant fairy tale was the last thing Carly expected, but it was absolutely something she could deliver.

"And I can do that. We can work together to create something that has never been done before, something uniquely you. I want you to look at the portfolio, but your cake isn't in here because it hasn't been designed yet. It'll be one of a kind, just like you."

"Ooh, I like the sound of that." Sequoia's eyes sparkled, and Carly forged ahead to close the deal, hoping that Michael would realize what was happening and keep his mouth closed. While Carly struggled to start her own business, Michael had already published a cookbook and shot a pilot. It wasn't picked up, and he eventually returned to Dallas to open his own bakery, but from what she could tell, he was an instant success. His moderate fame from *Sugar Shock* and the cookbook translated into big business back home.

"Maybe these are a little too out-there for your wedding cake." Carly indicated Michael's more daring flavor samples. "But people love something new and exotic for a groom's cake, and I'd be more than happy to work with you to create that."

"We can do something fancy and elegant for the wedding cake, and Rusty can do whatever crazy combination he wants for the groom's cake? That sounds perfect to me!" The bride clasped her hands together and nodded decisively. "What do you think, honey?"

"What?" Her groom looked up from the portfolio, his mouth full of gingerbread cake. "Whatever you want, baby doll."

"Great, then you two are hired. When can we get started?" Sequoia pressed her hands together on her lap and bobbed a little in her seat, clearly excited by the possibilities.

Carly's delight at being hired on the spot for such a huge job fizzled when she realized what Sequoia was saying. She and Michael weren't a package deal. They didn't work together, she didn't want to work together, and she didn't want him anywhere near this wedding. Determined not to freak out, she focused on retaining her professional persona. "On a job this size, you'll be my first priority. Simply let me know when you're available, and my staff and I will be there. I want to make sure everything is perfect for your big day." She pulled a manila folder from her bag and passed it to Sequoia. "If you would review and sign the agreement, we'll get the process started."

Michael looked like he wanted to interject, but Carly shot him a look and shook her head the tiniest bit. She would offer him something to get him to concede later on, anything he wanted, so she could have the account. There was no way he needed the work as badly as she did. Besides, if the bride wasn't on board, he had no chance of getting the job anyway.

Sequoia's pen hovered over the agreement. "I can't wait to get started. I want to do the cake, maybe a dessert bar, probably something for the bridesmaids' luncheon. I'm so glad we found you. I hadn't thought about trying to find a couple to work on the cakes, but here you are. It feels right, you know? Like it's meant to be. It's going to be so great!"

"You mean me and him?" Carly waggled a thumb between herself and Michael.

Sequoia's brow furrowed in confusion. Obviously the message that two companies were pitching during the same appointment hadn't reached her. "Are you two not together?"

Michael closed the distance between them and slung an arm over Carly's shoulder before pressing a kiss to her temple. She ignored the way heat shot through her at the casual contact, and forced herself to focus on the job instead of remembering the last time his lips had touched hers. His voice rolled over her, the words sounding so natural she almost believed them herself. "Oh no, we are definitely together. We just try to keep things professional when we go out on a job. You must be very perceptive to pick up on our relationship."

Sequoia visibly relaxed and looked pleased with his reply, scrawling her signature on the agreement as she spoke. "I guess when you're in love, you can see it in others as well. I want to surround our union with love and light, and I think it's important that the dessert that represents our marriage is baked with love, not infused with negative emotions or loneliness."

"Oh, sure. I think you're absolutely right." Michael was close enough that Carly could feel his warm breath against her cheek, and an unwelcome shiver skipped down her spine. What were they getting themselves into?

Sequoia was well known for her quirky beliefs and her odd proclivities. She'd joined Rusty on tour and had cleared entire rooms when she felt the staff projected negativity. It wasn't unusual for her to rearrange furniture or nix decorations if she thought a room's energy flow was off. But pretending to be a couple was a bit much. Carly pasted a pleasant smile on her face and gazed at Michael with adoration while they packed up their samples. As they wound through the crowd, she maintained the ruse, even going so far as to accept a playful pat on her rear without so much as flinching.

Once in the hall, with the door safely closed behind them, Carly put some distance between them and snapped. "What the hell were you thinking?"

To her consternation, he laughed. "I was thinking that we should do whatever it takes to get the job. Why is the thought of pretending to be with me so disgusting?"

"Is everything a joke to you?" He'd acted the same way on *Sugar Shock*, and it still annoyed her.

"Of course not, but I don't see the harm in going along with this one little thing if it means we get the job."

"If *we* get the job? *We* don't work together, Michael."

"Looks like we do now, cupcake, unless you want to go back in there and tell them they need to find someone else. I don't know if you noticed, but Sequoia seems to have made up her mind that she needs a couple in love to work on her wedding cakes. Maybe you don't care about the exposure, but I do. This could lead to major work in the future, and if it means pretending that we're together, that's a small price to pay."

"But it's lying." Hearing it out loud made Carly realize how weak her excuse sounded.

"So don't lie. All you have to do is pretend you don't cringe at the sight of me, and we'll be fine. This is one job, and then we can go back to never seeing each other again. It's not like Sequoia's going to ask if we want to double date with her and Rusty. Just follow my lead and relax. I've got this covered." His green eyes twinkled with amusement. Once again he was completely at ease while she was up in arms.

She put up her hands in surrender. "Fine. I'll go along with it, but only in front of them. Don't get any ideas."

Michael stepped closer, invading her space, reminding her of that one idiotic kiss they'd shared. As he tucked a tendril of hair behind her ear, he murmured, "What makes you think I'd get any ideas?"

"I don't know. Just don't." She walked toward the elevator, leaving him standing alone with that cocky smirk on his face. She hated that he still rattled her. Hated more that her heart raced as his voice wound its way around her like a warm breeze.

Chapter Two

Michael followed the muted strains of Pachelbel's "Canon in D" into the workroom after the girl at the counter of Caketopia waved him back. He found Carly perched on a barstool at her immaculate stainless steel table. Her tongue poked out between her lips and her eyes were narrowed in concentration as she piped elaborate lacy designs onto a sheet of wax paper. Working at her table, oblivious to everything else, she looked softer, approachable even. He'd always thought she was attractive—with her beautiful auburn hair, those expressive blue eyes, and that amazing honey-smooth voice—but her rigid, proper exterior made him keep his distance. The kiss they'd shared during *Sugar Shock*, the one that should've changed everything between them, only made her more determined to hate his guts.

He watched for a moment, lulled by the soft music and her precise movements before clearing his throat. "Doesn't this music put you to sleep?

He laughed as she jumped, pushing out a blob of icing and nearly toppling off the stool. The way her cheeks flushed as she smoothed her hair back and struggled to regain her composure stirred something inside of him. If only she let her guard down more often. She was so much more appealing when she wasn't trying so hard to keep everyone at arms' length.

"Sorry, cupcake. Did I scare you?" He walked in and stopped at her side, studying the designs she was referencing and practicing. He preferred a more freestyle approach to cake design, and wondered why she spent so much time practicing when she could be creating.

"I didn't hear you come in. I've been too focused on getting this design right." She set the piping bag down and angled her body to face him. "I like the music. It's beautiful, and it puts me in a wedding mood, but it's not the only kind I listen to. What's up?"

"I thought I'd drop by so we could figure out how we're going to work this job together." He waved his hand toward the door. "Your place is really nice. Very, uh, neat." His own storefront was more like a clubhouse, and his clients loved the wild outlaw atmosphere. His workshop looked a lot like Carly's, scrupulously clean and meticulously organized, but it was closed off to the public. All the better to project his carefully cultivated reputation and make visiting his shop feel like an experience.

Her blue eyes narrowed as she looked up at him, her lips pursed ever-so-slightly, and he found himself wondering if those lips still tasted like sugar. Probably. Or maybe some other plain, classic, boring wedding cake flavor. "So, since you decided to lie and create this sham relationship, we have to work together now. I don't really see why you couldn't have called."

"Come on. We're going to have to get along, so why not start now?"

"We have to get along in front of Sequoia and Rusty. Otherwise, I don't see why we can't keep our distance. The more I think about this, the stupider it seems. We should've just come clean and let them decide who they wanted to hire."

"You saw Sequoia's face. Once she decided that she wanted to work with a couple, there was no changing her mind. You know as well as I do that if we had told her the truth, we would've both walked out of there without the contract."

She sighed with a little groan, a sexy but infuriating sound. "You may be right, but I still think I could've done it on my own. She obviously wasn't interested in a Michael Welch original creation." Coming from her lips, his name sounded like something you scrape off the bottom of your shoe.

"Why do you say that like it's something that smells?"

She shifted on the stool and hooked her feet over the rungs. "I just mean that not everybody is dazzled by your flashy, crazy ideas. Not everyone needs a celebrity baker, you know. A lot of people still recognize quality even if it hasn't been splashed all over TV and magazine pages."

"So now it all comes out, what you really think of me. And here I thought we could get along." He leaned on her table, getting closer to her and enjoying the way it made her squirm. "We did once, remember?"

"I'll have no trouble getting along with you. I just don't know why we had to throw pretending to be together into the mix. Don't worry, though, I'm a professional." Her prissy manner raised his blood pressure, but he still wondered what she'd say if he pulled her off that stool and kissed the smug look right off her face. What was going on? This chick clearly thought he was a joke, so why couldn't he stop thinking about tasting her smart mouth?

"What's that supposed to mean?" God, she was infuriating.

"Nothing at all. I would have preferred it if you hadn't started this charade, but since you did, I'll go with it. I'll be professional."

"Well, so will I, regardless of what you probably think." He leaned over and stopped with his face just inches from hers, enjoying the way she shied away from him. "What I really want to know is why you find the idea of being with me so repugnant." She smelled like vanilla and sugar up close, and Michael's body was responding to her in ways the ice princess probably wouldn't appreciate.

Carly turned so that he couldn't see her eyes when she spoke. "It's not repugnant to me. I just know that I'm not your normal type, and it feels like a joke."

"I don't have a normal type, cupcake." He hadn't seriously dated anyone in years. She must be thinking of the vapid B-list wannabes who glommed onto him for a chance to get their pictures in the paper. The same women who would drop him like a bad habit if they got the chance to be seen with someone with more star power. The kind who lost interest once they found out what his private life involved more than just fun and parties.

Her blue eyes flashed when she looked back at him. "Whatever you say."

With her fire and confidence returning, things got much more comfortable. His attraction to her was making him uneasy, and he was likely to do something stupid if she let her guard down enough to allow it. Michael steered the conversation back to business.

"Have you talked with the blushing bride again?"

"She sent me an email a couple of days ago outlining everything she was interested in so we could get some ideas ready for them. I was just playing around with the lace design, but I have some bigger ideas too. She wants, and I quote, 'something elegant, magical, unique, and like a fairy tale.' Should be easy enough, right?" She laughed, but it sounded nervous to him.

"We'll nail them down when we meet with them again in person. Don't worry about it. I get the feeling Rusty will go apeshit over any wild idea I toss out, so I should have time to help you if you need it."

"Since this was supposed to be a one-person job, I'm sure I can handle my part on my own. Let's just make the best of this ridiculous situation we've been forced into." That vulnerable woman he'd glimpsed a moment ago was long gone, replaced by the same stuck-up princess he'd surprised in the elevator. The one who needed a stiff drink and a good lay.

"If you'd just remove that stick that's lodged in your ass, this could be a fun gig, not something we have to make the best of."

He stormed out of her workroom, sick and tired of her uptight attitude, and headed for the door. His phone rang, interrupting his rambling thoughts.

"Michael Welch?" the unfamiliar voice asked.

"You got him." He continued down the hallway to the front of Caketopia.

"This is Eric Macintosh with *Sugar Shock.*"

That stopped him in his tracks. "Hey, Eric, how's it going?"

He searched his memory to match the name to a face, but could only remember a production assistant who hit on all the show's female contestants. Staff changed on those shows all the time, though. Maybe he had been promoted.

"Great, thanks for asking. Listen, we've heard that you and Carly Piper are an item and that you're doing the Rivers-Grainger wedding. Any truth to the rumors?"

Michael glanced toward Carly's door, wondering if she was listening. "Yep. We are, and we are."

"Awesome. We would love to have the two of you come out for a guest appearance on this season of *Sugar Shock*—possibly to judge a portion for our Valentine's Day episode? It's short notice, but we wanted to get you out here before the season is over. First we heard that two former competitors were a real-life couple, and then we found out that you're working one of the biggest weddings of the year! We couldn't wait to get involved. What do you think?"

Michael scraped his hand over his chin, knowing that Carly would flip. Exposure like this was too good to pass up, though. Surely she needed it, and he was always interested in working toward making Michael Welch a household name. His shop was a big local success, his cookbook a steady, if modest, seller, but he wanted more. His pilot hadn't been picked up, so if he could get another shot at a show, he'd be set. There'd be more books, a product line, maybe a proprietary method class. The sky was the limit, but he had to take opportunities as they came.

Before he could change his mind, he answered. "We'd love to. What do you need us to do?"

A few minutes later, Michael walked back into the Carly's workroom and knocked on the doorframe, knowing he should've checked with her first. She'd be pissed at the least, refuse to go at the worst, but he had to bite the bullet and tell her. Then she looked up from her work, and it didn't matter how irritating she'd been earlier; the slightest bit of heat passed between them when their eyes met. This was ridiculous. If there was any chance she was softening toward him, that would be blown once he opened his mouth again.

He cleared his throat. "Hey, I just got an interesting phone call from the producer of *Sugar Shock*."

Her back straightened, and she went still. "And?"

• • •

Carly tucked a small bottle of her favorite perfume into her cosmetics bag and set it on top of a stack of panties in her suitcase. Her best friend, Lily Ashton, quirked an eyebrow in amusement. "Planning on getting lucky?"

Carly wrinkled her nose. "No, of course not. Don't be ridiculous."

"Those are some fancy panties for someone going away on business. I'm just saying."

Carly couldn't explain why, but she wanted to look her best when she was with Michael in Los Angeles. "This whole thing is ridiculously stressful. I thought it might be easier to face if I looked and felt my best, that's all."

"I totally get that. What I don't understand is why you're pretending to be Michael Welch's girlfriend. I thought you hated that guy." Lily ran her fingertips over the perfume bottles on Carly's dresser before picking one up to sniff.

"I don't hate him, but I don't exactly like him. We got caught up in a lie during the Sequoia Rivers and Rusty Grainger pitch, and somehow ended up posing as boyfriend and girlfriend." She combed her fingers through her hair, wondering again why she'd let things go so far.

"What are they like? Is Rusty as cute in person as he is on television?" Lily perched on Carly's tufted pink vanity bench.

She shrugged. "Yeah, he's pretty cute, but not my type at all. He was way too impressed with Michael. He seems like a real guy's guy, you know. I wouldn't be surprised if he ends up with a groom's cake shaped like a monster truck or something. Sequoia Rivers was interesting, though."

"She's kind of earthy and spiritual, right? Did she read your tarot cards or something?"

Carly laughed. "No, but now that I think of it, I'm surprised she didn't. She was really insistent that the wedding cakes be made by a couple in love, because emotions infuse themselves into food or some such nonsense."

"So that's how you got yourself into this mess." Lily slicked gloss onto her lips and pressed them together as she watched herself in the vanity mirror.

"I thought about coming clean, but I need this account too badly. Any time I think about backing out, I just imagine how much business will pick up after we do the wedding. I think it could lead to more high-profile events and celebrity weddings. If nothing else, I won't have to worry so much about money every time something breaks." Carly tucked the last t-shirt into her suitcase and zipped it closed. "It does feel like things are getting out of hand, though."

"I know you think he's a jerk, but I wouldn't mind letting things get out of hand with that guy. He's super hot." Lily was a drop-dead gorgeous model who could certainly have Michael if she wanted. Carly wondered what he'd say if he got a look at her. "And he seems like the kind of guy who knows his way around a bedroom. *IF* you know what I mean."

"The last time I let things get out of hand with Michael, I ended up getting voted off the show, remember? One minute, I was telling him about how worried I was that my childhood stutter would come back if I got too nervous, and the next minute, he was throwing me off my game by kissing me silly. So no, I don't want to find out if he knows his way around a bedroom. I already know he'd make a horrible boyfriend." Carly wrinkled her nose. She and casual sex did not mix, and she was lucky she hadn't let things get too far the last time. She'd almost let herself believe that he was the kind of guy who could be right for her when they'd shared that stupid kiss. Then he'd gone back to the competition like nothing had changed, continued to make her look like a loser, and before she knew it, she was going home.

"Who said anything about a boyfriend?" Lily waggled her eyebrows comically.

Carly threw a ball of socks at her friend. "This is serious, Lil. It was bad enough when we just had to pretend in front of people to get a wedding contract. Now we're going on television? I'm in too deep." She swooned dramatically.

"Who knows? Maybe you two will fall in love for real, and you won't have to pretend anymore." Lily's giant brown eyes were sincere. Lily had already found her Mr. Right, and she was a firm believer in true love. She'd married a young soldier against her parents' advice after a whirlwind courtship, sent him off with a kiss and a prayer to Iraq, and lost him eight months into his deployment.

Carly scoffed. "Ha! I doubt that. Michael's the last guy I'd choose as my boyfriend."

"Why not? He's gorgeous, talented, and smart enough to write his own cookbook. What's not to like?" Lily dabbed Chanel No. 5 on her wrists.

"You know I don't date guys like him. He'd have to show me that he's completely different now, and I seriously doubt that's going to happen. I need someone I can count on to be there for the long haul, not someone who shows up in the paper with a different blonde on his arm every other month."

"Well, there's nothing wrong with a good time, either. Not every guy has to be your soulmate."

Carly wasn't interested in finding her soulmate either, not after her last serious boyfriend had stomped on her heart and her belief in love along with it. Nicholas, the ex, had been a fellow baker at the shop where she'd cut her teeth on wedding cakes. He betrayed her with a quick and dirty affair with a bridesmaid. For icing on the cake, when the whole mess came to light and the irate bride confronted Carly, who was the lead baker on the account, Nicholas bolted for the door, leaving her to clean up the mess. If she ever fell in love again, it would be a miracle, and it wouldn't be with someone like Michael Welch. For her to take a second chance, the man would have to be unconditionally dependable and absolutely unlikely to break her heart.

"I'll be lucky to get through the trip without wanting to tear my hair out, to be honest with you. I'm pretty sure it won't be a good time."

• • •

Michael swirled the ice cubes around in his plastic cup and craned his neck around Carly to look out the plane's tiny window. Even miles away from her bakery, she smelled like cake, and he was surprised to realize that he was starting to like it. Starting to like her, even. She was more easygoing when they got away from work, and for once, every little thing he did wasn't annoying to her. Going on the show together obviously appealed to her as much as getting a root canal, but once everything came together, she'd relaxed a bit. The two fingers of whiskey she'd been nursing throughout the flight might have had something to do with it, but there was definitely a difference, and he wasn't about to question it.

"I would've pegged you for more of a diet soda type of girl." He pointed to her plastic cup of whiskey.

"Oh, you would." Her snide tone told him that the alcohol hadn't completely loosened up her distaste for him yet.

"Would what?"

"Assume that you know me. My father's part Irish, and though he's never actually set foot in Ireland, he fancies himself a whiskey connoisseur. I reserve it for heavy-duty situations, but I can definitely appreciate a good whiskey. Not that this qualifies, and if my dad knew I was drinking it out of a plastic cup, he'd disown me."

He laughed. "And now I know why you always make sure everything is just right."

That earned him a crooked smile. Now they were getting somewhere. "Yeah, I probably got my appreciation for presentation from him. He's an art conservator, so he's very particular, very detail-oriented."

"Well, it's been working for you. I don't know anyone else with the same eye for precision." He wanted to tell her how hot she looked without an apron hiding her figure, but figured he'd stick to something that wouldn't piss her off. She was finally loosening up a little, and he didn't want to ruin it just yet. "Have you watched the show since we were on it?"

To his relief, she laughed. "No. I don't watch a lot of television anyway, and *Sugar Shock* isn't really my kind of show."

"Why not? I thought we had a good time." The show had been an awesome experience for him, one of his favorite times in recent memory.

"I'm sure you did. It was probably a lot of fun for someone like you." She finished her drink and leaned back in the seat. The Carly he was used to, the one who thought he was an idiot, crept back into her voice. How did she manage to work an insult into every conversation?

"Someone like me?"

"You know what I mean." She waved her hand loosely in front of her. "Flashy style, edgy designs, always leading the pack. Someone who loves the attention, loves to bring the shock and awe with him." She giggled at her last statement, and even though she was making fun of him, it was pretty cute.

"Just because I don't use the same old white lace designs as everyone else or chocolate-covered strawberries decorated like tuxedos doesn't mean I do it for attention."

"No need to get defensive. You make what people like, and that's nothing to be ashamed of. For me, *Sugar Shock* was just another example of how I'm not what everybody wants." She shook her cup, jiggling the ice cubes against the plastic, and raised an eyebrow, so he flagged down the flight attendant and ordered her a ginger ale. It was still early, and with the time difference, she'd be in for a long day if she weren't careful.

"Cupcake, plenty of people are buying what you're selling." Himself, for example, which was a complete surprise. He could imagine what she would think if she knew. That was a discussion for another time, though. He'd figure that out on his own.

She blew out a sharp, hard breath. "Yeah, right. It's fine." She straightened a bit. "It just means that it's harder to stand out since I stick to classics. It doesn't make it any easier to get anywhere in this business or get my product line off the ground."

"I don't have my own product line." He kept his voice soft and light.

Carly faced him and leaned against her seat. A strand of auburn hair fell against her cheek, and he stopped himself from tucking it behind her ear. "Yeah, and why is that?"

"I definitely want one, and I'm brainstorming another book, but I'm not quite there yet. So far, the only product lines in stores are by people with their own shows. If I could get another show lined up, I'd have a better chance of it taking off."

A single guy who was already a huge success should have no trouble going after his dreams. When that same guy was tethered to his younger sister, circumstances were different. Nothing in life meant more to him than caring for Jenny, and he didn't resent anything he'd given up for her. There would never be a time when she wouldn't need him, and Michael had never met a woman who wanted to sign up for that life. He shrugged and hoped that the conversation would end there. No such luck. Carly's drink arrived, and she settled into her seat, curling her feet underneath her as she took a sip.

"It's been three years since the show, and you're still just as popular as ever. Even I have your cookbook, not that I'm able to duplicate everything in it. No other bakers I know of show up in the society pages with sexy dates. You're the only one." Her blue eyes watched him over the rim of her cup.

"I'd like more, but for now, the shop is enough." He drained his own drink.

"Still, you are a big enough name that it could happen, I'll bet." She pointed the air conditioner toward her face. She wasn't going to let it go.

"I don't mind waiting on the product line, and I'm perfectly happy at the shop. I get to do the coolest jobs of anyone in town. Besides, it's kind of fun being the big fish in a little pond. It suits me."

He paused. Carly sipped her drink and watched him, clearly waiting for the rest of the explanation. "All right, fine. The pilot tanked, and by the time I tried to find a business partner, it was too late. The cookbook sells pretty well, and the shop makes more than enough, but I can't see myself launching a product line or shooting another pilot. I can't afford to risk losing that much money, because I am responsible for my little sister."

Carly's eyes widened, and to his dismay, she looked surprised. She obviously had never considered that he'd be the type of guy to support his sister, and it was disappointing to him. "When I was eighteen, she was in a car accident with my parents. They didn't make it, but she did, thank God. I've been her legal guardian ever since. She has permanent brain damage and will need care for the rest of her life, so my responsibility didn't end when she became an adult. She's in assisted care, and my parents' insurance has paid for a lot, but I have to supplement it. I can't risk her future like I could risk mine if it were just me."

"Oh wow. I had no idea."

"I don't advertise it." That was an understatement, as he guarded her privacy fiercely, keeping her out of the spotlight and news stories about himself. Carly narrowed her eyes. Did she think he was embarrassed by Jenny? "My sister needs a lot of structure and routine in her life, and no stress. She can't handle a lot stimulus or noise, so I keep my life with her private." The reality of Jenny's needs had been too much for his only serious girlfriend, and Michael knew that most women would be no different. Relationships were hard enough without throwing long-term care into the mix. There was no point in getting serious with someone who couldn't understand that when he said he'd care for his sister for the rest of her life, he meant it.

Either content with the answer or finally picking up that he was done with the subject, Carly left it alone. Silence stretched out between them, interrupted only by the flight attendant stopping by to collect their empty cups, until the pilot's voice came over the speakers to announce their imminent arrival in sunny Los Angeles.

• • •

A petite blonde dressed head-to-toe in figure-skimming black met them at baggage claim. Valerie the production assistant introduced herself and then took off at a quick clip, throwing information at them while rushing through the terminal at warp speed, her long ponytail swaying with every step. Carly had never been happier that her luggage was on wheels as she struggled to keep up with Valerie's frenetic pace. They walked out into the warm weather and radiant sunlight for the briefest moment before sliding into the limousine's cool interior.

Carly scooted to the far end of the seats, and Michael sat right by her. His hand was warm on her bare skin as he squeezed the knee left exposed under her skirt. He filled the space between them with the easy confidence he was known for, and to her surprise she found herself leaning into his touch. The whiskey she'd had on the plane and the new revelations about his personal life both endeared him to her. They'd never been this close, and no sooner than she wondered why he was being so affectionate, Carly remembered they were supposed to be a couple in love.

The show was starting, whether she was ready or not.

Chapter Three

The charade continued when they arrived at their hotel and found that they had been booked into one room together. Staying in the same room as her boyfriend should be the most natural thing in the world, so Carly was careful to hide her surprise. Paparazzi filtered into the lobby as word spread that Michael Welch had arrived. In her self-imposed bubble, it was easy to forget that he was a big deal, especially in a town where even the most minor celebrity was a draw. Their season on *Sugar Shock* was one of the highest rated ever, and it wasn't because of her. The camera loved him, and he loved the attention.

Once they got away from the crowd, she would relax. Spending the night together would be awkward, but at least they'd be behind closed doors and could let their guard down. Surely Michael would be just as relieved as she would be when they were alone and could drop the ruse for a few hours. It might even be nice to spend more time together, getting to know each other. He'd surprised the heck out of her on the plane, so obviously there was much to learn about the bad boy baker she'd spent the last couple of years rolling her eyes at.

"If you two would like to settle in and freshen up, I'll pick you up in an hour. Just meet me in the lobby, and we'll head out. We have a dinner planned so the staff can brief you on the episode." The assistant scarcely looked up at them as she spoke, her attention focused on her cell phone where she was tapping out messages. "I have one quick little errand to run, and then I'll swing back by to get you." She strode away from the reception desk and out the hotel's doors without a backward glance, leaving Carly and Michael alone again.

"Here you go," said the front desk attendant as she pushed two hotel room card keys across the desk. "Let us know if we can do anything to make your visit more pleasant, and enjoy your stay." They were dismissed with a nod and a generic smile.

Cameras flashed and voices swirled around them as they made the short walk from the desk to the elevator, but Michael dismissed the crowd with a smile and wave. Once the doors closed behind them, the silence was deafening. If he felt awkward during their elevator ride and walk to the suite, it didn't show. His trademark swagger was front and center, his expression was relaxed, and his smile was easy. He spent a lot of time in the spotlight, either with his high-profile baking jobs or equally visible dates, so if Carly simply followed his lead, they'd likely be okay.

He unlocked the door, and she held her breath as she walked in to the suite, tempted to squeeze her eyes closed but holding them open to see what they'd be facing. To her chagrin, there were not two beds, but only one king size bed, smack dab in the middle of the bedroom, taunting her and reminding her why she was here. Its sumptuous linens and the room's beautiful accoutrements did nothing to quell her nervousness, and she looked longingly at a small sofa in the suite's sitting area. Perhaps it folded out, and she could crash there for the night. Surely he didn't think they would share a bed. Then again, he probably didn't feel the crackling tension and surprising longing she did when they touched. He probably wouldn't even think about her as a woman, would likely fall asleep without fretting about how close they were, unlike her.

As though reading her mind, he shot her a grin, which unfortunately sent a jolt of awareness straight through to her core. "Don't worry about a thing, cupcake. I won't try to pounce on you just because we have to share a bed." Surely, that sexy rasp hadn't always been in his voice.

"I was thinking I'd take the couch, actually." To her horror, she sounded prim and uptight, not breezy and casual like she'd intended.

He scoffed. "Don't be ridiculous. Between the traveling and the meeting, we'll be exhausted when we finally get to crash tonight and there's plenty of room for two. I'll be a perfect gentleman." Before she could protest again, his voice dropped an octave and he added, "Unless you don't want me to be."

She sputtered, her mind unable to form coherent thought through a cloud of lust and shock. "What?" *Oh, that was brilliant.*

His lips curved into a sly grin. "You heard me."

"Let's just get ready for this meeting." He was teasing her, and she couldn't allow herself to get caught up in some silly fantasy where they ended up together. Things were different between them because they were away from home, and she wouldn't start to believe in the illusion. Keeping work and romance separate was a good policy, and nothing had changed. She crossed the hotel room, giving him a wide berth. The sooner they got out of there, the better.

• • •

Carly relaxed a bit as she walked with Michael down the hall to the elevator, relieved to be out of the room and the uncomfortable intimacy of sharing such a small space alone. If her attraction to him was evident now, at least they were pretending to be a couple, and he wouldn't suspect her feelings were real. She joined him in the elevator and allowed herself the tiniest moment to enjoy his decadent fragrance, surprised at how luxurious and masculine he smelled. Like bergamot and leather. Delicious. As the doors shut, he closed the distance between them, and Carly let her handbag slip to the floor, as though hypnotized.

Michael was close enough to touch, so near that she could feel the faint heat radiating from his body, and his low voice rumbled through her. "Don't panic, but I'm going to kiss you."

"Oh." It was all she could manage, trapped in his orbit as she was. His eyes were like emeralds, sharp and brilliant, as she looked up to see the desire she'd been battling reflected on his face. Maybe if they kissed, she'd find that he wasn't as irresistible as she'd thought and her ill-advised attraction could be shelved. Wait, they had kissed, and it was a disaster last time. Though every piece of her begged her to lean in, she stepped back. "No you're not," she whispered, unable to find her voice.

He glanced at the floor buttons, lighting up one by one as they approached the lobby. "Listen, cupcake, when those doors open, do you want the paparazzi to see a couple in love or two game show judges?"

Well, he had a point, and as long as their boundaries were clear, there was probably no harm in one little kiss. She had a business to build, one that would only benefit from her fake celebrity romance.

"All right," she managed to consent.

Michael needed no further encouragement. Before she could catch another breath, her face was cupped in his hands and he was looking deeply into her eyes. This was much more intimate than she'd pictured, already more satisfying and romantic than the raw, animal experience she'd imagined. Her eyelids fluttered closed, and his lips landed on hers, soft and warm, tentative even. She snaked her arms around his waist, faintly registering how firm the muscles beneath his clothes were, and pulled herself against him. His hands were in her hair, and a low moan rumbled in his chest. Their breath intermingled, warm and full of possibility, and Carly raked her fingertips against his back, stopping herself short of pulling his shirt out of his waistband.

Realizing how close she was to following through on her fantasy, she pulled back enough to keep her hands to herself. The doors whooshed open, and flashbulbs went off. He was right. The paparazzi loved a show, and they'd delivered. Michael's lips curled into a satisfied smile and he dropped a soft kiss to her forehead before pulling her into his arms. She could hear his heartbeat with her face pressed to his broad chest, and she melted against him. Giving into her attraction wasn't the wisest idea, but she'd worry about what it all meant—and how to handle it when they were back in the real world—later. Surely once the ruse ended, her feelings would, too.

•••

Michael sat next to Carly at a table in a busy Mexican restaurant, surrounded by *Sugar Shock's* staff members, only a couple of which he remembered from their time on the show. The executive producer, Jules Miller, ordered pitchers of margaritas for the table and leaned forward on her elbows, eyes gleaming with excitement.

"So, when we heard that not only are you two working together on the celebrity wedding of the year, but that you're also an actual real-life couple, we just had to ask you back for an appearance. We couldn't resist the angle, of course, since you kind of hated each other on the show, but now you're clearly in love." Jules dipped a tortilla chip into salsa and took a tiny bite.

"It'll be fun to be on the show again. What exactly did you have in mind for us?" Michael gave his practiced showbiz smile to the producer.

"Our special Valentine's episode is coming up, and we'll have the current semifinalists doing either wedding cakes or something on theme for the holiday. We haven't finalized the plans yet, but the focus will be on romance. You two will stand in as judges for the episode."

A waiter arrived and passed out glasses for everyone, then took their orders as pitchers of margaritas were passed around. Chatter from the conversations swirling through the restaurant grew louder as the evening wore on. Michael inched closer to Carly, knowing that it might make her uncomfortable, but wanting to remain true to the image they were presenting. After he'd practically assaulted her with that kiss in the elevator, sitting close to him at dinner was probably child's play for her. While they chatted with producers, he put an arm around her shoulders and casually rubbed the skin exposed by her sleeveless dress with his thumb. Her cheeks flushed faintly, but she didn't shirk out of his reach for once.

Kissing her at the hotel was probably a mistake, and for the life of him he couldn't figure out why he'd done it. Sure, he told himself that the extra attention would help strengthen their story and bolster their appeal, but that was a flimsy excuse, one that Carly was sure to see right through. She was barely amenable to the charade as it was, and he'd taken one of the few safe places they had and swooped in on her like an overzealous frat boy. If they had any hope of making it through this trip without slipping up, he'd have to be more careful. The heat between them felt real enough, and she'd certainly kissed him like she meant it, but one kiss wouldn't likely change the way she felt. She'd made no secret of her opinion of him, and he'd have to disregard the wild attraction he felt for her.

"Will our decision be final?" Carly asked as she looked up and made room for the waiter to deposit her plate. She poked at rice and beans with her fork while Jules answered.

"We'll record a few different scenarios and use the one our regular judges agree with. Your comments and contestant feedback will be very valuable, but it's only fair to have consistency in the contest."

"So, it's all just for show? We'll be judging, but it won't count?" Her voice was casual, probably deliberately cool, but she speared a slice of avocado with more force than was necessary.

"It's not that it won't matter, but your appearance is more for content than for the competition portion. We thought it would be fun and romantic to have a couple that met on our show come on for the Valentine's episode. You two will be interviewed, both individually and together, and we'll try to find some good footage from your time here, that kind of thing. I'd like to highlight how much things have changed between the two of you since you met, so we're hoping to find some juicy clips. We wanted to catch up with contestants from past seasons, and having you two highlight your romance will be completely organic. That won't be manipulated for results, but the contest itself should be consistent."

"That sounds great." Michael hoped Carly would let it go without argument. They were in no position to judge a reality show, after all. He found her knee under the table and gave it a light squeeze. Her eyes closed for a second, and she leaned closer to him, accepting a light kiss on her temple.

"We'd like to get some footage of you two together outside of the episode as well. Do you remember Eric Macintosh from when you two were on?" So it *was* the same guy who had hit on all the female contestants. "He's busy this evening finalizing the plans for your dates out on location. He's a genius at finding the perfect situations for our contestants, so I'm sure he'll set up something amazing for you two." She took a bite of her dinner and dabbed her lips with a napkin.

It shouldn't be too difficult for them to act natural on a staged date, but after that crazy kiss in the elevator, Carly probably needed a chance to process what was happening. Surely she was still reeling from the shock of him pouncing on her and would appreciate a reprieve. They were clearly convincing everyone at the table that their relationship was real, but he didn't want to push her too far.

"I guess we could do that. What do you think, babe?" Whatever she was comfortable with, they'd do. They'd only agreed to appear on the show, so if she was really opposed to the date, he'd try to get them out of it.

"I wouldn't mind a low-key date, I guess. It's kind of weird, having cameras follow us outside of the show, but I'll do whatever we need to do." She sipped her margarita, and a tiny fleck of salt from the rim clung to her lip, making him want to lick it off.

The producer beamed. "Wonderful. We'll make the arrangements, and all you two need to do is show up tomorrow."

• • •

There was nothing left to do with their evening but retire to their suite, so there was no way Carly could avoid facing Michael alone any longer. No errands, no meetings, nothing could postpone the inevitable. For the past few hours, it had felt less like pretending and more like real-life, and if they didn't snap out of it soon, Carly wasn't sure she'd ever want to slip out of the charade. She reminded herself again that her attraction to him was influenced by his boyfriendlike behavior and would likely be short-lived. Once they were back home, he'd be back to the guy she loved to hate.

His hand landed at the small of her back, and she suppressed a tiny shiver as they walked toward the hotel elevators. As the doors closed, his hand dropped and he stepped away, giving her the space he probably thought she wanted. She couldn't let him know that she missed his touch as soon as he withdrew his hand, that nothing felt more natural. She let out a breath and mentally willed the elevator to get them upstairs faster. The sooner they were alone, the sooner they could drop the charade for the night. If only he wasn't standing so close. And why did it bother her that he was keeping his hands to himself during this elevator ride?

The hallway was blessedly empty when they arrived at their floor, and Michael unlocked the door and let them into the room without touching her again. He kept his distance once they were in the dim, hushed room, the air conditioner's soft whirring the only sound. As she watched him move around the room, completely at ease, she wondered why she'd let herself think that the kiss meant anything. He wasn't even looking in her direction as he picked up the remote control and dropped down onto the suite's little couch, his long legs stretched out in front of him. Michael absentmindedly flipped through channels, his eyes trained on the television screen, obviously unaffected by the situation. Closing her eyes briefly, she could remember his hot lips on hers, the way her body had instantly responded to him. She could even recall how his mouth had tasted of warm cinnamon. Now she wondered if it wasn't all her imagination.

Alone in the bathroom, she ran her hands over her body. How could she have thought that someone who literally dated fashion models would go for her? She was pretty enough, sure, but taste-testing everything came with the price of several extra pounds. Her hair was a gorgeous, wild shade of red, but it was stuck in limbo, its limp waves neither straight nor bouncy curls. Michael was tall, toned, and muscular. She was short, soft, and curvy.

Dressed in a modestly cut sleep shirt, and figuring she couldn't stall any longer, she tiptoed out of the bathroom, hoping to slip into bed without further discussion. Michael was talking quietly into his phone, engrossed in his conversation, and snapped to attention when the bathroom door closed behind her.

"Sorry. I didn't mean to disturb you." She cringed and hurried past him to the far side of the bed.

He smiled and held up a finger.

"She's here right now, Jen." He laughed. "Maybe I can get an autograph for you or something. Okay, I'll try to check in again soon, but you can call Aunt Jane if you need anything that can't wait."

Sitting up, he turned the television off, and Carly pushed away a fantasy of curling up on his lap. This was truly getting out of hand if the sight of him using a remote turned her on. "Good night, sleep tight." He ended the call. "That was my sister. I just needed to check in and make sure our aunt visited with her today. She doesn't necessarily need a visit every day, but I try to stop by anyway. It's a little strange for her when I'm away."

"Oh, that's sweet of you to do that."

"It's nothing, really. I don't want her to feel abandoned in the assisted living place. They have activities for her there, and she has her own friends and routine, but nothing can replace family. She was especially excited to hear that her favorite *Sugar Shock* contestant Carly Piper was here with me."

"What? She remembers me from the show? That was years ago!"

"She watches our season all the time." Michael grinned. "I'm pretty sure she thinks you should've won instead of me."

"Well, I can tell that she's a really smart girl. You should bring her by Caketopia when we get home. I'd love to meet her."

He stood and stretched, and Carly's heart sank at how quickly her eyes moved to the sliver of skin exposed when his shirt rode up. Knowing how warm and hard his body was, her fingers itched to touch him again, to have his lips pressed against hers. Summoning her last shred of dignity, she pulled the comforter back and slipped into bed, careful to stay as close to the edge as she could. When she'd thought he was a wild playboy, bent on using his celebrity to bed as many women as he could, it was easy to ignore any attraction. Seeing his devotion to family, as fierce and loyal as her own, was bad news. It made it too easy for feelings to develop, too easy to fall for a man who wasn't interested.

Michael lifted one eyebrow. "Do you think you're close enough to the edge?"

She scooted toward the center a few inches and attempted a confident voice. "Better?" If only she didn't sound so buttoned-up. He must think she was absolutely ridiculous.

"Do you want me to sleep on the couch?" To her relief and disappointment, he wasn't teasing her. She could handle the mocking, annoying Michael she knew. His respect and kindness was unnerving new territory.

Yes, please, sleep on the couch. "No, of course not. We're both adults, so I think we can sleep in the same bed without making a big deal out of it. Besides, we both need a good night's sleep before the big date tomorrow."

"Cool. I'll be back in a minute." He was casual, unconcerned with whether or not they shared a bed. She was the only one overthinking every little detail.

As he turned to walk toward the bathroom, Carly smoothed the sheets and comforter over her, stopping just short of tucking herself in. She blew a gentle breath up toward the ceiling, wishing that she could look away, but unable to force her gaze away from Michael's back. His fitted t-shirt moved against his muscles as he walked, driving her wild with curiosity about what that back looked like under the clothes. As warmth crept into her cheeks, she darted her glance away only to land squarely on his butt. The cutest butt she'd seen in a long time. If he came back out in anything but the rattiest, baggiest clothes, she'd be in trouble.

The few minutes it took Michael to brush his teeth and get ready for bed stretched out into an eternity. Carly couldn't decide if she wanted him to stay in the bathroom or come out and get it over with. If only he would make one of his cheesy comments or act like a pig or something. Anything. Just a chauvinist remark, something to put them back on familiar ground. Though now that she thought of it, Michael wasn't a chauvinist. He was cocky, larger than life, annoying to be sure, but he wasn't a bad guy. Now wasn't the time to realize that though. Now was the time to remember that this trip, this experience, was not real life.

The door opened, and he came out in loose sleep pants that hung low on his hips, and, Carly noted as her throat dried up, no shirt. Tucking the sheet up under her arms, she reminded herself to breathe as she took in his bronze skin, tapered waist, and muscles. How was it that he had a body like that, muscled and defined, while she actually looked like she taste-tested her work every day?

He moved around the suite, turning off lights, and shot her a sexy grin when he noticed her watching his every move. She cleared her throat and snuggled further under the blankets, wishing she could burrow underneath completely.

After turning off his bedside lamp, he slid under the sheets, close enough to touch. "Good night, Carly. Sleep tight."

"Good night." Surprised she was able to say anything at all, she closed her eyes and tried to relax. He was close enough that she could smell his minty toothpaste, close enough to feel the warmth from his body. There was no way she would be able to fall asleep.

Chapter Four

"Where do you think we're going?" Carly checked her makeup in a hand mirror as their car took them through Los Angeles traffic.

"I have no idea. I thought it might be something baking-related, but that seems kind of boring. These shows usually send contestants on things like helicopter rides or cave explorations or something crazy to make things more interesting, so it's anybody's guess. Don't be surprised if it has nothing to do with us, even though they said they'd match the date to our personalities."

"Well, whatever it is, the suspense is killing me." As was the close proximity to Michael in the backseat of the car. The cool air conditioning was the only thing keeping her from overheating in such close quarters.

"Try to relax and enjoy the last few minutes before cameras are on us. Save your energy for pretending we're a happy couple," he whispered, though the driver wasn't likely listening. His warm breath against her ear sent a shiver down her spine and had goose bumps dotting her arms.

"I think we did pretty good last night at the dinner, don't you? It seemed real, right?" She patted her neat bun, checking for rogue locks of hair.

"Absolutely. After that, today should be no problem. I mean, most of the people last night knew us when you hated my guts. If they can be convinced that we're a real couple now, today should be a cakewalk. We'll have to keep up appearances in front of the crew, but wherever they're sending us, people won't know anything about us. They'll have no reason to ask questions."

"You're probably right. I'll be glad when it's all over, though. All this pretending is exhausting." Not to mention excruciating, between grappling with her confusing feelings for Michael and hiding them from him.

"It's nowhere near over, cupcake. We've got to keep it up until after the wedding, too. Might as well buckle up and enjoy the ride." He grinned, his eyes crinkling at the corners.

They pulled into the parking lot of Angel City Italrican, an Italian-Puerto Rican fusion restaurant, and Carly sucked in a breath. Why couldn't they be pulling up to a place that actually had something to do with *Sugar Shock*? Why not a bakery or even a winery for a tasting or something? A studio tour would've been nice—anything but complicated fusion food.

Baking and cooking were completely different skill sets, and Carly was much more comfortable with the precise chemistry that went into baking than with the experimental, loose guidelines of cooking. Showing off her finished pastries was easy, but being watched as she put together a meal step by step was excruciating. The pressure to get everything perfect flustered her so that she made mistakes, stumbled over her words. The show producers either had a publicity deal with the business or were looking forward to placing them in an unfamiliar situation.

"Ah, so it looks like they've got a cooking show segment lined up. I'm actually surprised they don't have us doing something crazy." Michael shrugged, though he still looked cool and confident. He might not be an accomplished chef, but he didn't seem too worried about it. He'd probably take it in stride like everything else that came his way.

"Crap." She was a lot less calm about the prospect of walking into the restaurant and trying to act like she knew what she was doing.

•••

"Come in, come in, you beautiful people. I'm so glad you're here!" A tall, wiry, and very tan man greeted them at the door and whisked them into his orbit. His coal-black hair shined under the bright staging lights, and a gold tooth caught the light when he smiled. "I'm Antonio, and today, you are in my capable hands. We're going to have a wonderful time together, so I hope you are ready for some fun in my kitchen."

The production crew bustled in behind them and set up around the otherwise empty restaurant. Michael took Carly's hand and followed Antonio further inside, their shoes squeaking on the polished floor. She was clearly nervous; her body practically thrummed with tension. He squeezed her hand and gave her what he hoped was an encouraging look. Whatever happened, he'd do his best to help her get through the segment without making a fool of herself. Neither one of them could cook for an audience, apparently, but he wouldn't let the segment turn into a joke at her expense.

"Carly, Michael, tell me. Have you two beautiful lovers tried anything like my restaurant before?" Antonio laid a hand on each of their shoulders, enveloping them in an Old Spice-scented cloud.

Carly still looked like she might throw up, so Michael took the lead. "No, can't say that we have. You'll have to be gentle with us."

Antonio grinned. "It'll be so much fun. You'll see. I've cooked for hundreds of people, and I haven't lost anyone yet."

Antonio left them to confer with the production crew, and Michael held Carly by the shoulders. "Are you okay?"

"I just hate stuff like this." Her shoulders fell. "I'm going to look like an idiot."

His touch clearly relaxed her, and he loved it. Nobody besides his little sister reacted to him like that, like he was someone you could count on, and he wouldn't take it for granted. "Listen to me." He took her chin in his hand, gently, and tipped her face up to look into her eyes. "You aren't going to look like an idiot. This is for television, remember? You're going to come off like an old pro, and look sexy as hell doing it. Follow my lead, and you'll be fine."

The trust on her face nearly broke him. Had he just made a promise he couldn't keep? It might be smarter to grab her hand and make a run for the door, but he would hang tough. This was the one time he could be the dependable one, and he wouldn't waste the chance. Besides, once their trip ended, he'd be out of opportunities to hold Carly in his arms.

Antonio crossed the room to meet them, light on his feet and beaming with enthusiasm. "Carly, Michael, I have your aprons."

Antonio gave them each aprons emblazoned with the restaurant's logo across the front. Carly turned so Michael could tie hers in back, and he had to stop himself from running his fingers along her spine.

He wasn't nervous about cooking or making a fool of himself. Baking in his private workroom was a far cry from cooking a romantic meal for an audience, but he was hardly an amateur. Though he'd prefer to do it with cakes, commanding a cooking show was exactly what he wanted to do with his life. This could be his chance to prove himself, to show the Cuisine Network execs that he deserved another chance. With any luck, Antonio would do most of the talking, and they'd be there for show. If they completed the cooking segment without looking like fools, he'd consider it a success. Playing the hero to her damsel in distress was immensely appealing, and he was warming to the role. Truthfully, he couldn't wait to see her in action, to watch her cook.

With a hand at the small of her back, he leaned close, close enough to smell her light perfume, and murmured in her ear. "This will be fun. You'll be amazing."

She turned to face him, her forehead skimming faintly across his lips. "I don't know about that. I hope he won't expect us to teach the audience how to make the dishes."

"I can't imagine that he would. They didn't set this up so we would look like idiots."

She crinkled her brow and looked away. "I can do that on my own."

With gentle hands on her arms, Michael held her until she met his gaze. "This is supposed to be fun, but you might as well be about to defend your dissertation. What's really going on?"

She shrugged out of his grasp. "Nothing. I just get nervous when I have to talk for the camera like I know what I'm doing."

"But what about *Sugar Shock*? And what about our interview for the show tomorrow?"

"That's different. When we were on *Sugar Shock*, I was just completing the challenges or talking to an interviewer. I don't mind if it's candid or something I actually know how to do. I can answer questions. I just don't like looking into the camera and talking about something I know nothing about. It makes me nervous."

He lowered his voice as a staffer approached with their microphone packs. "Let me take the lead when I can, then. We'll get through this together."

Carly adjusted her apron and took a steadying breath. "Okay, let's do this. Do I look all right?"

"You look like a goddess." His voice caught on the last word, and he swallowed hard.

Her cheeks reddened, and she walked around him toward the man carrying their microphones. He'd meant to encourage her, not embarrass her, but the words slipped out before he could think. As he watched her walk away, Michael tried to think about baseball, term life insurance, organic broccoli futures, anything unsexy. Anything but what those curves looked like under that apron.

"Pardon my reach," the production assistant joked as he snaked the microphone wire under the bottom of Carly's shirt and out through the collar. "All right, there you go, Ms. Piper. You are wired for sound and good to go." Now that the microphone was turned on, they could hear and record every word they said.

Antonio breezed back over. "The crew is all set up and ready to roll camera. Are you two beautiful people ready to cook?"

• • •

They followed Antonio into the makeshift studio, where the crew had set up bright lights, cameras, and boom microphones around the perimeter. They stopped in the middle of the kitchen island, where Antonio was staging the area with bowls, utensils, and foods.

"You two have never cooked together?" Antonio asked. They shook their heads. "How can that be? There is no better way to express your love for another than to create and share a meal together. Today we will learn to cook some of my favorite dishes, and you will love it. We'll have a wonderful time."

Carly looked to Michael, breath catching in her throat. The snow-white shirt he wore beneath the apron set off his perfectly bronzed skin, and the top few buttons were left undone to reveal just enough to make her want to see what was underneath again. His dark hair was gorgeous, thick and shiny, practically begging for her to run her fingers through it. He always wore tight skullcaps at work, and she'd never really noticed how touchable his hair was. They needed to get to the cooking, and quickly.

"All right, now Michael, if you and your beautiful Carly will each add your spices to your meat, we will get started on one of my signature dishes, Spanish meatballs."

Antonio took a small remote control from his pocket and pointed it across the room. Lively salsa music filled the space as he adjusted the sound and swiveled his hips in time to the song. "Okay, we take the traditional meatball from my papa's Italian childhood and give it some flair from my sainted mama's Puerto Rican culture."

They tossed garlic, cilantro, and finely diced tomatoes into their meat mixtures before adding eggs and seasoned homemade breadcrumbs. Antonio hummed and danced in place to the music, explaining the steps along the way.

"Growing up, my home was always filled with music, especially when we were in the kitchen." With hands on Carly's and Michael's shoulders, he encouraged them to begin. "Now, we get our hands dirty. Get in there and knead the ingredients together."

Carly and Michael plunged their hands into the bowls, mixing the ingredients as they laughed. As long as she wasn't giving the instructions, the cooking was actually fun. It felt like they could be standing side by side together in her kitchen at home. They formed bite-sized meatballs and placed them on wax-paper-covered baking sheets Antonio set before them. Antonio cleared the counter and prepared the ingredients for the next dish as they left him to wash their hands.

Antonio continued talking to the camera, giving viewers the instructions to finish the meatballs, as salsa music drifted through the kitchen. Michael hummed as he dried his hands, his hip bumping against Carly gently in time with the sensual beat. She glanced up from the sink to see that he was looking down at her, his expression heated. With an exaggerated flourish, he swept her into his arms, pressing his body against hers. His hips swiveled as his feet completed basic salsa steps. Though her first instinct was to slip out of his grasp, she found that being enveloped in his sexy bergamot scent was too good to resist. Before long, her feet mirrored his, and he was whispering in her ear.

"One, two, three. Five, six, seven." Even numbers sounded sexy when they rumbled across her earlobe from his lips.

"How do you know how to dance like this?" she said breathlessly.

"It's a secret." She could hear the smile in his voice, and the way the word sounded coming from his lips made her curious about what else he could do.

Caught up in the moment, she forgot to be self-conscious, forgot that she wasn't a dancer. She let him lead her around the tiny kitchen space behind the main area. It didn't matter if Antonio saw, or if the cameras captured their dance. Nothing mattered but the spark between them and the way it wound through her body like a lit fuse.

"Yes, yes, that's it. Beautiful!" Antonio encouraged them as they danced around the kitchen. "Perfect, you two! Why didn't you tell me you were dancers?"

Being pulled into Michael's orbit, seeing him in his element, clearly in charge of the situation, made Carly wonder where else he would shine when he took the lead. The song came to an end, and Michael improvised, twirling her around in his arms and dipping her low. His strong arms held her at her waist and shoulders, and as she struggled to catch her breath, he kissed her softly before pulling her back to her feet. The dance, the heat of the set lighting, the kiss—it was all too much.

"That was beautiful, you two. Your talents are clearly wasted here in my kitchen," Antonio said with a smile. "What a lovely pair."

He was right, but Carly knew it would be over too soon.

• • •

Blessedly, Eric Macintosh didn't join them on the drive from the restaurant to the next mystery location. Being stuck in an enclosed space with him would probably give Michael a migraine. When they were on *Sugar Shock*, Eric made sure all the female contestants knew that he was open to using his influence in exchange for favors. At the time, it was irritating. Now that Michael was getting closer to Carly, feeling more protective of her, it was infuriating. She looked tired as she dropped her head back onto the seat. After cooking together, dancing together, fitting together so perfectly, it was easy to imagine that their relationship was real. It would be so natural to lean over and drop a kiss onto her forehead or move closer so she could rest against his shoulder. It was all too real, but he didn't want to snap back to reality just yet.

"There was a series of dance lessons for residents at my sister's facility." He'd never shared so much about his life with Jenny, but Carly seemed to want to know.

"What?" She sat up a bit, roused from her drowsiness.

"That's where I learned to dance. Jenny didn't want to at first, but I talked her into it because learning new things is good for her. The only way she would do it was if I took the lessons, too."

"That was sweet. You're a good brother." Carly's casual observation hit home. All he wanted was to do right by his sister. Most of the women he knew considered Jenny an inconvenience at best and a burden at worst, but Carly was different.

He cleared his throat and changed the subject. "You look tired, cupcake."

"I am, but I'm sure I'll rally when we get to the next location. I hope it's low-key, though. I'm exhausted."

"I hope so too, but you never know with *Sugar Shock*." She pointed out the window, and Michael realized they had parked in front of a microbrewery. "Looks like it's our lucky night. The only thing I love more than a good whiskey is a great beer."

Eric hurried across the parking lot to meet them as the camera crew spilled out of their van. "Hope you like beer, guys." The cheesy grin on his face said otherwise.

"We love it, Eric. Excellent choice." Michael answered and watched Eric's grin fade with great pleasure. The skeeze likely thought Carly preferred fruity cocktails or something. Guys like him seemed to enjoy nothing more than throwing women off-balance.

"Great. We've got a brief tour scheduled, and then you two can settle in for light snacks with beer pairings." Eric walked across the parking lot and held the door open for them. Michael was careful to stay between her and Eric.

The brewmaster met them in the empty bar and restaurant section. "Welcome to Amber Wolf Microbrewery. I'm Steve Monk, the fool who started this whole thing." The crew got to work setting up cameras, lights, and sound equipment. "I'll give you two a brief tour of the brewery, and then you'll enjoy our food and brews here at the bar. I have some of our seasonal and limited-edition brews on tap for this evening, all of which are excellent, if I should say so myself."

They followed the brewmaster past swinging doors into the brewery. "I opened Amber Wolf just five years ago, and we've grown by leaps and bounds. We're already the largest independent copper tank brewery in California." He led them across spotlessly clean concrete floors toward giant copper vats and tanks. "Here, we're brewing a single-hop Belgian-style pale ale called White Liberty. It's light but complex, with a crisp bite. Very popular, especially this time of year as we're moving out of winter and looking toward spring." They wandered to the next copper vat. "Here's my personal favorite, Jubilee Lager. Other places would reserve this for the winter months, but I took a gamble that there are other beer drinkers like me who enjoy a full-bodied lager year-round. It's a dark lager with cinnamon and vanilla undertones, and we actually rename it and sell it in souvenir growlers during Christmas. Shh, don't tell anyone it's the same stuff we serve year-round." He grinned at Michael and Carly, clearly pleased with his practiced spiel.

As Michael and Steve got involved in a discussion about brewing, he noticed Carly wander off with another staff member to chat about flavor profiles and label design. The portly bearded man grew animated as he talked about his craft, and she watched him intently, smiling and nodding. From the precious few times Michael had received that shining focus, he knew that the guy was in heaven. When Carly listened to you, it was as though you were the most interesting person in the room. Her focused attention probably made it possible for her to create her intricate wedding cakes, but it was softer, sweeter, when targeted at a person. He watched them walk, wishing more than anything that he was that beer guy.

Steve cleared his throat, and Michael snapped to attention and whirled around to face him. "Sorry, man. I guess I was a little distracted." He nodded toward Carly and shrugged.

To his relief, the brewmaster laughed rather than taking insult. "She's a looker, bro. Guess I can't compete. Is that your girlfriend?"

No, she wasn't his girlfriend and she never would be, but for the duration of the trip, Michael could pretend that he belonged at Carly's side. "Yep. She's all mine."

"Lucky man. So these are my custom-fitted copper tanks ... " Steve continued the tour as Michael smiled and nodded, replaying the salsa dance in his mind on a loop. Full-bodied brews in copper tanks couldn't compare to the full-of-life beauty with copper hair who felt like heaven in his arms. He could still smell her, could hear her voice if he closed his eyes.

Steve paused and nodded behind Michael. "Looks like you're not the only guy with eyes for her."

Michael glanced over his shoulder and saw Eric Macintosh practically caging Carly in between a wall and his body. Everything he'd heard about Eric's treatment of female *Sugar Shock* contestants flashed through his mind, and he could only imagine what he was saying. Without a word to the brewmaster, Michael stomped across the facility. Carly was pressed hard against the brick wall, scrunched as far away from Eric as possible. Her eyes darted around the room until they settled on Michael, and she visibly relaxed. For a second, he felt like he'd found his home in her eyes, and it looked like she felt the same way.

Eric touched Carly's arm, and her relief disappeared as she stiffened. His voice was low, but Michael was close enough to hear. "I've got an inside track on a pilot the network is developing for the new season. We could talk about it, see about getting you an audition." He ran a fingertip down the length of her arm. "What do you say? Want to get out of here for a while?"

Michael's instinct was to grab Eric by the arm and fling him off of her, but he wanted to stay with Carly, not spend the night in jail. Eric was behaving like a creep, but he wasn't threatening her, so physical violence was out of the question. With a huge effort, Michael stuffed his anger away and approached them. "Hey, cupcake, sorry I got caught up with that guy. He really knows his stuff. You ready to get something to drink?" He took her hand and nudged his arm into the space between Eric and Carly, brushing against Eric's smooth silk shirt, holding his breath to avoid the cloud of body spray.

She slipped out of Eric's grasp and practically flung herself at Michael, gluing herself to his side. He pressed a kiss to the top of her head, and she gazed up at him, giant blue eyes grateful for the reprieve. For once, the adoring look was likely genuine. No matter what she thought of Michael, at that moment, he was her hero. "I can't wait, baby. See you later, Eric."

They left the brewery and pushed through the doors to the restaurant, arm in arm, Carly clung to him so tightly that Michael wished he could rescue her every day.

He dipped his head until his lips were almost touching her ear. "Are you okay?"

She nodded as she slid onto a barstool. "Yeah, he was gross but not scary."

So she didn't want Eric's attention, but maybe Michael had been a bit abrupt, a little too protective. "Cool. I saw the way he was blocking you in and thought you might need help getting away."

"He definitely doesn't take a hint, that's for sure. The more I made it clear I didn't want to have anything to do with him, the closer he got. I can't tell if he's a jerk or just doesn't know when to stop. Either way, I've never been happier to see you coming my way." She grinned, and he found himself grinning back.

"Well, then it looks like I should buy Eric Macintosh a drink."

"Definitely." Carly shifted on the barstool and picked up a menu after the bartender pushed two frosty glasses of beer across the bar.

Michael watched Carly sip the lager, her lashes fluttering closed as she savored the cold drink. "It's good to finally sit down."

"Yep. I'll probably fall asleep as soon as my head hits the pillow."

He cleared his throat and studied the menu, uncomfortably reminded of the bed they'd be sharing later that evening. The more time they spent together, the harder it was to respect Carly's boundaries and keep his distance. They ordered dinner and chatted about the brewery, a welcome distraction from the tension he felt.

The ever-present microphones were a welcome addition during their meal. At least while they were on, he could treat Carly like his girlfriend, could say anything he liked and she wouldn't balk. He dipped a French fry in ketchup and fed her, watching her lips as she accepted it. Aware that the camera was trained on them, he took advantage of the moment and kissed her, softly, her jaw cupped in his palm.

Leaning close enough to smell her shampoo, he paused and watched the pulse jump at the base of her neck before whispering in her ear. "This is much more fun than our first time on the show together."

She laughed, the tension broken, and nodded her agreement. "Definitely."

They finished dinner as the crew got their final shots of the brewery, and then left for the car, trailed by a camera man. In the low light of the setting sun, Carly was luminous. Bolstered by their comfortable evening together and frankly unwilling to resist, Michael cupped her face in his hands and kissed her. Her eyes stayed closed for a moment after he pulled away, and the longing that pulled at his heart was nearly unbearable. She was perfect, but she wasn't his, and this wasn't real.

Chapter Five

A sliver of soft early morning sunlight peeked around the edges of the hotel room's blackout curtains at the perfect spot to hit Carly's face. She squeezed her eyes shut against the light and groaned as she snuggled closer to Michael. Tucked in where she fit perfectly, with her forehead skimming his jaw and her chin resting on his collarbone, her lips were close enough to his neck to kiss. She breathed in, letting his scent fill her senses, and snaked her arm around him. Spending the day wrapped in his arms would be perfect. He mumbled in his sleep as he turned his head, his stubble catching in her hair, and her eyes flew open.

Why was she in Michael's arms? He'd saved her from that creepy encounter last night, so now he was her savior? As quickly as she could without waking him, she scooted to her side of the bed and smoothed the blankets over her, creating a firm barrier. A quick glance beneath the sheets told her that she was fully dressed, and a brief scan of her memory reassured her that the only thing they'd done in bed last night was sleep.

It was a wonder she'd even been able to fall asleep lying beside him. As she listened to his breathing become heavier, steadier, and still, she practically vibrated with tension. Exhaustion won out eventually, giving her a few hours of precious rest.

She must have found her way to him subconsciously as she slept, her body acknowledging what she'd worked so hard to ignore. Had he woken to find her pressed against him? Did he feel the same sweet perfection in the way she fit in his arms? With any luck, he wouldn't realize that they'd spent the night wrapped up in each other. He stretched in his sleep, flinging one muscled arm over his head and the other over her stomach, and her heart sank. There was no denying how beautifully they fit together, how natural it was to be at his side. If she didn't clear her head soon, didn't remind herself in no uncertain terms that they were here on a job and these feelings weren't reciprocated, she'd end up getting hurt.

Today, they'd return to the *Sugar Shock* stage to complete their interview, and she was sure to screw it up somehow if she didn't get her head straight. With a gentle touch, she moved Michael's arm off her stomach and slid out from underneath the blankets. As quietly as she could, she padded around the bed and across the room, hoping to get showered and dressed without waking him. She sent one last glance toward the bed before closing the bathroom door, where he lay bare from the waist up, eyes closed but with the hint of a smile on his lips.

• • •

Back on set, Carly stood still as a production assistant snaked her microphone wire through her clothes and hooked her up for the interview.

Across the room, Michael was laughing with another production assistant, clearly comfortable and in his element. His broad shoulders were relaxed; his face held no hint of uncertainty. Lord, he was handsome. He had a lot more experience in front of the camera than her, but her nerves weren't about being filmed. After yesterday's date at the restaurant, she was certain she could handle anything they threw her way. But the microphone she wore meant that the *Sugar Shock* staff would hear everything she said once it was turned on, and she'd have to be more cautious than ever if she didn't want to spill their secret. Most of the material they shot would be culled and tossed, but there was a chance she'd slip up and say something to Michael that would give their deception away. Being alone with him was nerve-wracking enough.

As his own battery pack was secured at his back, Michael's shirt rode up, and she caught a glimpse of skin. When had she become this wanton woman, drooling at the merest sliver of male skin? When she finally tore her eyes away from his midsection, she was mortified to see that he was watching her, a mischievous glint in his green eyes. He grinned at her, shooting longing straight to her gut, and her mouth dried up. This was going to be a long day. She cleared her throat. "Excuse me, can I have some water, please?"

The assistant nodded and left, and Michael crossed the room to join her. Even his walk was sexy today. This was truly ridiculous. "You ready to do this?"

She swallowed and nodded. He ran his hands down the length of her arms and gently took her hands in his, making it difficult to find her voice. "Sure, no problem."

"You seem a lot more nervous today than you did yesterday." His eyes reflected the concern in his voice. "This should be nothing compared to the cooking demonstration."

"I guess I'm a little nervous about saying the wrong thing, and I thought we'd prepare more. At least yesterday, if I messed up, it wouldn't mean that our whole story could crumble. It would just mean that I don't know how to cook. What if we contradict each other and the whole thing unravels?" She bit her lower lip and let her gaze wander around the crowded studio. She could get lost in Michael's eyes, and it was time to keep her wits sharp.

"It will be fine. Just remember that we're here so they can capture a love story. They just want to boost ratings. They're not looking to catch us in a lie or anything. Nobody's on trial here. All you've got to do is relax and pretend that you like me. Follow my lead if you get nervous. I won't let anything go wrong." There it was. She could count on him to guide them through the day's interview, and his confidence would carry her through. It was a relief to know that she could depend on him.

"I know you're right. It'll be fine." She nodded, summoning her confidence and wishing she had an ounce of his. He was, unbelievably, enough of a gentleman not to mention how she'd curled up against him and practically nuzzled him that morning, but she couldn't push her luck. The cocky, obnoxious Michael she'd come to know could resurface, ready to make fun of her.

"I think they'll have us sit together for the interview. I'll try to answer first if they ask anything too specific, and you can go with whatever story I throw out there." He grinned. "If I touch you or steal a kiss, do me a favor and don't flinch. You've got to act like you like it."

She laughed, sounding nervous to her ears. He certainly didn't flinch when she touched him. "I think I can handle it."

His gaze grew heated. "That practice kiss in the elevator was a good idea, huh?"

She swallowed, hard, and nodded. Again, where was her voice? "Yep, that helped." she squeaked out.

He glanced around, then lowered his lips to her ear. "You're so wound up this morning. Too bad we don't have time for another one. I think it would loosen you up." His breath was hot against her skin and smelled like cinnamon. She flashed back to her own breath against his skin, her face pressed against the dip where his neck met his shoulder. The sheer perfection of their fit, the peace she felt waking up in his arms, was intoxicating. And dangerous.

She stepped back, putting distance between them before she swooned. As much as she wanted another one of his soul-shaking, earth-moving kisses, that was the last thing she needed. She remembered the kiss they'd shared the last time they were on *Sugar Shock*. The kiss they never mentioned. She'd always let her emotions run rampant, foolishly, and needed to keep her expectations firmly grounded in reality. Another kiss would likely do nothing but set her imagination on a wild ride, and she'd only be hurt in the end.

Clearing her throat, she straightened her spine and smoothed her hands over her dress. "I'm going to be fine. They want a happy couple? Let's give them a happy couple."

She smiled brightly at an assistant who brought her a bottle of chilled water and accepted it gratefully. The PA flipped the switch on her microphone and then on Michael's as she drank from the bottle. It was show time. "All right, you're all set. Don't try to take your mics off without me or another staff member. I'll catch you after the show and get you undone. I think they're ready for you."

He left them alone, and Michael stepped closer. As his fingers entwined with hers, he pressed a kiss to her temple. She melted against him, turning her head to catch his lips with hers as though they'd kissed hundreds of times. Before she had a chance to question what had happened, he shot her a look and cut his eyes toward the show staff. The host was striding across the room towards them, and Michael was already in character. Carly stepped back and cleared her throat. It was time to get it together before she blew their story and ruined the whole thing.

"Michael, Carly, so nice to see you again!" Shelley Peabody enveloped Carly's hand in hers and squeezed, a warm, television-ready smile on her face. "Thank you so much for agreeing to do the show. We're so glad to have you."

"It's good to be here, back where it all began," Michael answered smoothly. "Carly and I keep up with the show every season, and we're really looking forward to meeting the contestants."

Carly hadn't watched a single episode of *Sugar Shock* since her season, but she smiled and nodded, summoning her enthusiasm. Shelley continued. "So, we're going to have the two of you over there." She motioned to a set with a couch, soft lighting, and a decorated table. "I'll be interviewing you, but I'll be off camera for that. Try to give your answers in a way that includes the question, like with the individual confessional interviews from when you were on the show. We'll splice everything together in edits and use what we can for the Valentine's Day episode."

"Sounds good," said Michael.

"So, just relax and enjoy yourselves. We're going to weave together the interview, footage from your time as contestants on *Sugar Shock*, and some scenes from yesterday's date, which from what I saw was amazing. When it's all said and done, your segment will be maybe fifteen or twenty minutes long. Nothing to stress about."

Michael slung an arm around Carly's shoulder as they approached the set. The hot stage lights warmed the entire area around the faux living room, and production staff milled around the area as they settled on the couch. She shifted and struggled to keep her breathing even as Michael sank down next to her. She didn't expect him to cling to the edge, but her mind had trouble functioning in such close proximity. Warmth from his body radiated toward her along with his delectable scent. This close, under the bright lights, she drank in every detail, from the faint stubble on his cheeks to the golden flecks she'd never noticed before in his green eyes. He flashed her a quick smile, revealing perfect white teeth and reminding her how that mouth felt on hers. She swallowed, her throat suddenly dry.

The cameraman rolled the camera to the center of the set, and Shelley seated herself on a canvas director's chair opposite them. "We've reviewed a lot of past footage from your season. I'm sure it's much fresher in my mind than in yours, but anything you can answer will be helpful. Like I said, it's going to be edited to death before it airs, so don't worry if you don't remember everything. Just try to relax, be natural, and have a good time."

Carly could only imagine what Shelley would bring up from their time on *Sugar Shock*. She and Michael had not only been competitors, they had practically been enemies, always sniping at one another or arguing. She was sure at least half of her confessional videos mentioned something annoying or obnoxious he'd done, and when she thought back, all she remembered was constantly being angry while he always laughed it off. Whenever the crew gave her an opportunity to air her feelings about Michael, Carly had taken it and run. They'd probably spin it during editing to make it look even worse. Contrasting their volatile past with their copacetic present would make for some great television.

Shelley leaned forward and began. "America watched as the two of you competed for the *Sugar Shock* crown, and I've got to say, we were surprised to hear that you ended up becoming a couple after the show ended. Tell us how that happened."

Michael shifted next to Carly and put his hand on her knee. "I'm sure plenty of people wonder how we managed to get together after what they saw on the show. When Carly and I were on *Sugar Shock*, we didn't get along." He laughed and squeezed the knee, his hand large and warm on her. "We were always at each other's throats, always fighting. It was like oil and water, man, and it was rough. You all saw it. That was then, though, and things have changed. The clashing," he bumped his knuckles together, "changed to sparks, and we've been going strong ever since."

"It does seem amazing that things have changed between us so much since the show. The day I got voted off, I was ready to leave just so I could get away from him. I didn't even care that I lost. I just wanted to get out of here." Carly patted Michael's thigh and laughed.

"Aw, come on honey, I'm not that bad, am I?" His easy endearment tugged her heart.

"Not now, of course, but yeah, back then I wanted to get away." She hated remembering how poorly she'd treated him, but he was taking it in stride. He always did.

"Then I'm sure you were just thrilled when I showed up to see you at your shop." Michael's eyes danced with amusement, and Carly got their contrived story straight in her head: that he'd come across her bakery by accident, and when they saw each other again, they hit it off.

"Oh, my gosh, that day was crazy." Carly smiled up at him and continued. "Things were going great. I had just opened this bakery back home called Caketopia. People recognized me from *Sugar Shock*, which really helped get things off the ground. Everything was perfect, exactly what I'd always hoped for, and then one day Michael Welch walked in the door."

"And I guess she wasn't happy to see you?" Shelley interjected.

"'Horrified' is how I would describe the look on her face when I walked in." He laughed, but Carly cringed. He'd always been cocky, had annoyed her from the moment they met, but she'd been awful to him. He was simply enough of a gentleman to laugh it off. Of course, they were on camera, so for all she knew he might still resent the way she'd treated him. That she'd never once considered how her overt nastiness affected him was shameful.

"But that's all in the past." She put her hand in his and gazed at him adoringly. The torture of having him there, just out of her reach, she could manage. Admitting that she wanted more and forcing him to let her down easy? Utter humiliation.

"So, how did you end up as a couple?" the host continued. "You were rivals on the show who opened up bakeries in the same city. How did you go from hating each other to falling for each other?"

They couldn't very well say that it all started as a charade to win a big wedding contract. Things had moved so fast since they pitched their services to Rusty and Sequoia, and even faster since they'd arrived in Los Angeles. It was hard to know how to answer. Fortunately, once again, Michael swooped in and led the way.

"When we reconnected, I tried to keep my distance at first. Only because she didn't like me, though. If I'd had my way, we would've mended fences and become close right away. I thought she was a little high strung, but I liked her."

"You did?" Carly searched his eyes, unable to find a hint of deception in their gorgeous green depths.

"Sure, cupcake. You were probably too irritated with me to notice, but I thought you were smokin' hot and really talented." His smile was as sweet as the sentiment, and in that moment she wanted to kiss him. Heck, she wanted to keep him.

"So, would you say you always liked Carly?" Shelley urged him to continue.

"Sure, I always liked Carly. I guess she didn't always appreciate my personality, but I thought our back and forth was spicy. At first, I'll admit it was fun to get under her skin. I mean, it was just so easy to get her worked up that I couldn't resist. She was always so uptight, so proper, that it sometimes felt like a game to see how far I could push her." Michael laughed as Carly rolled her eyes, then cleared his throat. "After I'd been in town for a while, though, she got better at avoiding me, and that's when I realized how much I wanted her. We worked in the same town but rarely crossed paths. We don't exactly attract the same clientele. I watched her interact with clients, saw how much care and professionalism she puts into every project, and started to admire her style more. It's so different from mine, you know, and I used to think she took the safe route when it came to design, but now I see it for what it really is." He paused and gave her a quick look full of adoration. "Classic and sophisticated, just like Carly."

"Wow. If I remember correctly, Carly, you didn't feel anything like this for Michael, at least when you were shooting the show. In fact, I know a lot of our viewers will remember you throwing a piping bag full of bright-blue buttercream icing at Michael on an episode." Shelley grinned at the laughter that erupted from the crew and audience. "When did things change for you?"

Michael's admission that he'd always liked her, and even come to respect her, was a shock, but Carly had to keep her head straight. He didn't need a script to say the right thing, and he didn't necessarily mean a word he said. Now was not the time to let her feelings get out of control.

"Honestly, the day he walked through the door of Caketopia, I wanted to get away from him so badly. I thought he would be the same as he was on the show, and I wasn't at all interested in finding out if I was right." To her relief, Michael gripped her hand and laughed. She continued, glad he was amused rather than offended.

"I actually remember the exact moment things changed for me. A friend told me a story about an employee of Michael's who had lost her husband. This woman was having a hard day, as she sometimes does, and I guess nothing was going right for her. Although the shop had more work than they could handle, he went to her. My friend told me that he just helped her get through the moment, as though the work could all wait until she was ready. That he was so gentle and kind without being patronizing. He had always seemed like the kind of guy who thought everything was a joke, but when I heard that story, I just fell for him. Right then and there. I saw him for the sweet, caring individual that he really is, that behind the jokes is someone you can count on. The rest is history."

He squeezed her hand, and she swallowed against the lump in her throat. Things were going too far, becoming too real. She had no such friend and had heard no such thing, but the story came to her when she thought about how gentle he was with his sister. He guarded Jenny's privacy so carefully that Carly knew better than to give the real example, but the feelings were close. Too close. They were too real, and she was in for heartbreak when they were finished with the Grainger-Rivers wedding.

Chapter Six

The four semifinalists, two women and two men, stood nervously in front of their creations. Carly and Michael sat at the judges' table, watching the contestants' expressions and waiting for production to resume. She leaned forward on her elbows and dipped her head as he whispered in her ear, reveling in the freedom of letting her attraction to him show.

"I think I already know which one you'll pick." His breath against her skin was delicious, as was the kiss he pressed to her temple. The cameras were rolling, but she didn't have to fake her cozy reaction as she leaned in closer to him.

"Did you get a sneak peek?" The cakes were still hidden behind dividers several feet away from the table where they sat.

"I took a little look behind the curtain. There's a Carly Piper wannabe in the mix."

"A wannabe? We'll see." Carly grinned at him, glad to not have to moderate her emotions. She was supposed to be in love with Michael, expected to gaze at him all googly-eyed. Hiding it from him later would be hard enough. She might as well enjoy the freedom to indulge in her attraction while she had it.

"We'll see when I'm right." His low laugh rumbled as she forced her attention to the host and contestants.

The director called for quiet on the set and counted down from three before the area was plunged in darkness. Spotlights then illuminated the judging table where Michael and Carly sat, and each individual contestant. Shelley Peabody walked toward the contestants, her face serious, as though she dreaded the task of sending contestants home. Carly hadn't made it this far when she was on *Sugar Shock*, but Michael had. None of the current season's semifinalists had a fraction of his talent. They stood by their wedding cakes practically shaking under the scrutiny, with no hint of Michael's easy confidence.

Shelley faced the camera. "Welcome back to *Sugar Shock*. Our guest judges are eager to see this season's top four semifinalists, and we know you can't wait either. So let's see what they've got for us this week." At her cue, the dividers were whisked away, and the studio audience let out a collective "Ooh."

Four distinctly different styles were reflected in the semifinalists' cakes. Carly's eyes immediately went to the traditional design that Michael surely thought she would pick. Without meaning to, she picked apart its flaws and quickly dismissed it as her choice. She took in the modern, boxy cake on the cart next to it, admiring the smooth work and sharp lines, but decided that it was dated and nothing that would interest most modern brides. The third cake looked like a Michael Welch copycat, with wild turquoise icing and uneven stacks of geometric cakes that looked as though they would topple over on a breeze. The fourth was deceptively simple, a white cake with smooth lines and exquisite detail. Subtle use of pale pastels in a pearlescent gum paste caught Carly's eye.

"Michael and Carly, what are your first impressions?" Shelley waved her hand dramatically past the contestants.

Michael cleared his throat and stood, eyes darting from one cake to the next as he stepped towards the carts. The contestants flashed him hopeful smiles. The show would use their comments, but Carly knew that their votes didn't affect the show's outcome. The real *Sugar Shock* judges would have the final choice, so whatever Michael and Carly thought really didn't count for much. Did the contestants know that? Like everything else in this charade, appearances were all that mattered. He turned to her, green eyes shining under the stage lights, and held out his hand. She swallowed down the lump in her throat and joined him. Her hand felt small in his as he laced his fingers through hers.

"I think I know which one you'll like, baby." Carly's heart raced as he led her to the cake she'd picked to win and stopped. She could pretend her feelings were as fake all she wanted, but Michael was coming dangerously close to making her fall for him. "It's a classic, but better, just like you."

Carly hid her nervousness and offered him a sweet smile. "This is amazing work, and I completely agree."

They walked to the Carly-wannabe presentation and paused. Carly tried to soften her voice, to offer praise within her criticism. "This cake is lovely, really, and I doubt a client could find fault in a single stroke of your spatula. The design is classic, traditional, and beautiful. Your work is technically proficient and nearly flawless."

Her next words would wipe the smile from the baker's face, and she hated to have to continue.

"However, there's something missing. There's no passion or originality in the design, none of that indefinable spark, that special something that makes your work unique. Perfection is a great quality when it comes to cake, don't get me wrong, but it's not everything." The young woman smiled bravely at Carly's comments, but unshed tears shined in her eyes. "It's a beautiful cake, and you do gorgeous work. You're very talented, but I'll be casting my vote for another cake. Good luck to you."

"My beautiful girlfriend is sharp, Shelley. I definitely see similarities between Carly's work and this one, and it makes me like it. I have to agree with her, and it doesn't get my vote, but I can see a lot of potential here and think you can have a great future."

"Moving on, then, which other contestant would you send home today?" Shelley directed them towards the remaining three contestants, moving the segment along.

"I don't know about Carly, but my choice is this one." He walked over to the modernist design. "I see what you're going for here, and I respect it, but I can't remember the last time we did a cake like this. We do a lot of weddings, and this kind of severe design is outdated. Technical perfection will only get you so far. To find success on your own, you've got to learn how to straddle the line between following the trends and putting your unique spin on design—to know and respect the market. In my opinion, you should take some time to really think about what you want out of your career and what you'll need to do to get there."

His advice was probably painful for the young man to hear, but Michael was spot on. For someone whose reputation was built on bucking trends and surprising people with outrageous designs, it was strange to hear him speak so logically about the industry. Michael knew more about successfully navigating the system than he let on.

"So is it safe to say our remaining two contestants are your choice for finalists?" Shelley's perky voice interrupted Carly's thoughts.

"I think so. What do you think, cupcake?" To anyone else, the endearment was sweet, but Michael had been calling her cupcake long before their charade began.

"Yes, I think these two are exceptional, and either could take the *Sugar Shock* crown."

The two remaining contestants presented wildly different, completely opposite, styles. Carly could guess which way the final vote would swing. The cocky young Michael clone would likely take the top spot, and once again, shock and awe would win out over posh quality. Ironically, only a fraction of real-world weddings featured wild designs. Almost all the brides who contracted with Caketopia went with more traditional designs, only branching out with slight variations. Michael won the contests, Carly did the work. Not unlike the relationship charade. Carly toiled behind the scenes to make the ruse seem real while Michael glided along effortlessly on the surface, contributing the flash and heat. She'd resent him for that, but the heat was becoming irresistible.

Chapter Seven

"I'll pick you two up tomorrow afternoon, so please meet me in the lobby by three so we can make it to the airport in time for your flight back home." Valerie the PA was already tapping a message on her phone before Michael or Carly could agree. She was gone in a flash of blonde hair and tapping keys without another word.

"Great, then we'll see you right here tomorrow," Carly responded, though the assistant didn't wait for their answer.

Michael slung his arm over Carly's shoulder and kissed the top of her head. "Hey, what do you say we have a bottle of wine sent up from room service? I think we deserve it after the last couple of days. We can celebrate making it through the show relatively unscathed." The only witnesses to their interaction were the hotel staff milling around the area, but they couldn't drop the charade until they were safely behind closed doors.

"That sounds great." It sounded perfect, actually. But in the face of his complete ease, she was loath to admit how unnerved she was by their kiss and her apparent one-sided attraction to him.

They walked to the hotel bar, and he picked up a wine list. "What would you like? Red? White? Anything look good to you?"

He tilted the menu for her to see, but she couldn't focus on the individual listings. "Red would be fine, maybe a pinot noir. You choose."

"All right," he agreed with a smile, his eyes sparkling in the bar's dim light. She'd miss this, the easy affection between the two of them when they had to put on a good show.

Michael placed an order with the bartender to be sent up to their room and took her hand before leading her out of the bar. Keeping up appearances in front of production staff was stressful, but it was nothing compared being alone with Michael and not knowing how to act. It had been so much easier back when she couldn't stand to be around him, when she knew exactly where things stood. Now, she struggled to find a balance between letting her growing feelings show and hiding them. He didn't appear to have any such qualms, and he comfortably led her across the lobby, hand in hand, toward the elevators.

The metal doors closed behind them as he pressed their floor button and stood silently beside her, his expression neutral, pleasant, and infuriating. She was practically crackling with need, with want, and knowing that she couldn't get carried away. Tension strummed between them. How could he not feel that? It was practically electric. As usual, he was cool and confident, not bothered at all by their proximity or the huge secret they shared. She was ready for something to happen, anything that would put her out of her misery.

Without warning, he answered her unasked question with a kiss, swift and searing, and a longing that matched her own.

Unable to silence the satisfied sound that escaped her throat, she leaned into the kiss, and leaned into him. With her breasts crushed against his chest, she reached up to run her fingers through his dark hair, pulling him closer to her as she nipped lightly on his bottom lip. He smiled against her lips, mischievous and sexy. The elevator doors whooshed open, and without preamble Michael swept her up and over his shoulder, like a sexy caveman. Carly protested but giggled, loving how light and feminine she felt in his arms as he carried her to their suite. Had he seen a photographer? Or did he feel the same as she did?

He held her steady with one large, capable hand, right on her butt, while he fished the room key out of his pocket and stepped into the suite's cool darkness. As the door clicked closed behind them, he set her down gently before pushing her against the wall. He held her hands in place above her head as his mouth claimed hers in a deep kiss that left no further questions about his feelings.

She responded, meeting his enthusiasm with her own, as the lust she'd been fighting enveloped her and clouded her mind. Michael dropped her hands, and she plunged her fingers into his soft hair, luxuriating in the decadence of his kiss as she held him closer. His hands skimmed across her shoulders, down her arms, and around the swell of her hips before sliding over the curve of her backside.

A knock at the door snapped her attention back to reality. Michael laughed softly as their breathing returned to normal, and adjusted his pants. They hadn't made it more than a few feet inside the room, so he only had to turn to open the door for the room service attendant. Carly made her way into the suite and perched on a plush red sofa while he collected their wine and tipped the attendant. Before she had time to fully recover her wits, they were alone again and Michael was pouring a glass for each of them. He dropped onto the couch beside her and handed her a glass, his smile easy and inviting. She sipped, watching him over the rim of her glass, and struggled with what to say next. Why was he always so comfortable? Her nerves were working overtime, but nothing about what was happening seemed to surprise him in the least.

"What would it take to get you to relax around me?" He'd called her out, but his tone was kind. Gone was the cocky man who'd say or do anything to get under her skin. This was the new Michael, the one who turned her on, treated her with total respect, and made her feel safe. This new development was tricky to navigate.

Realizing she was sitting ramrod straight on the edge of the sofa, she moved back and forced herself to at least appear more relaxed. "I guess I don't know how to react to, uh, what's been going on between us."

"I like how you've been reacting." His lips curled into a suggestive smile, and he sipped his wine. "I really have enjoyed it, you know." The sincerity in his voice sent a shiver of pure feminine pleasure skipping down her spine. How did he manage to be rakish and sweet simultaneously?

She cast her eyes down at her lap, where her hands were gripping her glass. "I have, too."

"Then why are you trying to put as much distance as possible between us?" He scooted closer to her on the couch until their thighs were touching. "You seemed comfortable enough being close to me this morning." So he had realized that she had spent the night in his arms.

She sighed and wrestled with how to answer his question. "I don't know. Maybe I just need time to think about what's happening. I don't want to get caught up in something I'm not certain about."

"What's to be certain about? I like you, you like me. We have a good time together. Why not enjoy it while it lasts?"

"I'm usually not so … casual." She was never casual with her relationships, but something about Michael made her want to throw all her rules out the window.

"This is only as casual as you want it to be. If you'd rather cool things down, I won't push you. If you want to keep your distance when we're alone, I'll respect that. We only have to pretend to be together when we're with the production staff. But I can't be the only one who realizes how amazing it would be for us, right? Waking up with you in my arms this morning was damn near perfect."

It was too perfect, too real, and she didn't want to talk about it. Once her feelings got involved, once things moved beyond physical attraction, she'd be sorry. It would get too complicated, and she'd be left with a broken heart. Was it possible to suspend her growing affection for him, to simply enjoy the night? Maybe she could separate her emotions and her physical desires. Play it safe and stay away from relationship territory.

"One thing I can't seem to forget is that kiss from the first time we were on the show." She sipped her wine, worried that she'd revealed too much, let her real feelings show.

His brow furrowed. "Yeah, what about that?"

"It's just been on my mind this whole time, and I don't like pretending it never happened."

"We don't have to."

"Every time I think about it, I remember how bad things got between us."

"And you think it was because of the kiss?"

She shifted, not sure she wanted to get into the discussion. After a deep breath, she blurted out what she'd been hiding: "I hate the way it made me feel. I wanted to kiss you, but it was stupid to want it, and even stupider to do it. I knew the second we went back on set that you just wanted to push me off-balance, and I felt like an idiot for falling for it."

Finally. It was out in the open, for better or worse, and they could move on. The softening in Michael's expression was the last thing she expected. He cleared his throat and shifted in his seat, his gaze focused on her. "I wasn't trying to do anything but kiss you, Carly. There was no game. How could you think that?"

Speechless, she looked away, feeling a blush creep into her cheeks. Finally, she whispered. "I don't know."

"Listen, when we go back, we still have to pretend to be a couple, at least until the wedding's over. It won't be so difficult at home, you know, without a camera crew and people asking us about the relationship all the time, but we'll have to keep it up." He sipped his own wine, and his eyes danced with mischief. "Once we're alone again, you can go back to hating me or ignoring me or whatever you want. But just because we've had a rough start doesn't mean it always has to be that way."

"Maybe I'm overthinking this." He was clearly game to explore their compatibility without worrying about emotions getting in the way, and the idea was too tempting to dismiss. "Being together here is like being in a bubble, like who we are at home is irrelevant. I just don't want to do anything we'll regret later."

"I won't regret anything we do together." He leveled her with a serious look, a look that challenged her. A look full of promises she'd like for him to fulfill.

Whoa. One thing was sure, she'd regret letting this moment go to waste. It had been years since she'd felt connected to a man so completely, on such a primal level. The look in his eyes promised a night she wouldn't soon forget, and for once she threw caution out the window. She took a deep breath and stepped outside her comfort zone. "Let's just see what happens, then, and worry about what it all means another time. While we're here, anything goes."

"Come here." He set down his wineglass and patted his lap.

There was no turning back now.

Chapter Eight

Carly stood on trembling legs before him. Michael's eyes raked up and down her body, taking her in, clouding with lust. He centered himself on the couch and shot her an expectant look as he patted his leg, and she looked away, embarrassed. She'd always been too self-conscious to enjoy sitting in men's laps, and he was well-known for the twiggy women he usually dated.

"I want to see if what's under that dress is as gorgeous as I imagine." His voice shot a hot wave of lust through her. "It was so hard to resist finding out this morning."

A flush heated her face as she fingered the hem of her stylish, and figure-flattering, sleeveless A-line dress. What the hell, why not? She wasn't trying to become his girlfriend, and if he didn't like what she had to offer, he would simply move on. This was one night, probably the only one she'd ever have with Michael, and then they'd go back to normal. With any luck, once the mystery was gone, she could go back to breathing normally around him again, could look at him without swooning every time their eyes met. Once he saw what was hidden beneath her clothes, he might realize she wasn't what he was looking for. But he'd obviously enjoyed what he'd been able to feel through her dress. There was magic in the way he kissed her. Undeniable, spellbinding magic. There was something between them, even if she didn't know what it was.

"Unzip me." She turned her back to him and held her breath, hoping he'd stand to unzip her dress and not laugh at her failed attempt to sound sexy. She needn't have worried. Within moments, her dress was pooled around her ankles. She was more thankful than ever to have put on pretty, matching lingerie.

"Gladly." She heard the smile in his voice as he sucked in a breath and ran his fingertips lightly over her body.

His hands roamed over the fronts of her thighs and skimmed her stomach. Mindlessly, she pushed back against him, feeling very clearly just how interested he was. He fisted one hand in her hair and pulled her head to the side, gently and slowly, so he could drop kisses from her shoulder up to her neck. His lips were soft and warm, sending shots of pleasure to her core every time they made contact. With a groan, he turned her around, and out of habit, her hands flew to cover her stomach as she sucked in her breath. He raised an eyebrow and took her wrists in his hands, gently moving them to her sides.

"Don't hide yourself from me. I've imagined this so many different times, in so many different ways. Don't deprive me." He claimed her lips in a crushing kiss, hot and filled with longing. He urged her lips open and deepened the kiss as his arms encircled her, pulling her close until nothing but scraps of fabric separated them. "I've been dying to see what's under your clothes, and I don't want to waste a minute."

His lips left a scorching trail of kisses down her neck and across her collarbone. She ran her fingers through his hair, encouraging him. He sank onto the sofa and pulled her with him until she was straddling his lap. With fumbling fingers, she hurriedly unbuttoned his shirt, finally about to touch him without worrying about what it meant. What she found did not disappoint. His skin was smooth, soft and inviting, and she ran her hands over the planes of his stomach to find hard muscle bunched underneath. He was gorgeous, and for once, she'd simply take what was offered to her and forget about the consequences.

Was this wise? Surely not. Was she going to do it anyway? Michael picked her up and carried her across the suite to the bed, tossed her down, and unbuckled his belt. Yes. She was going to do it, and she'd love every second. His wicked smile told her that he had no reservations about what they were about to do. He pulled his belt through the loops and watched her, his searing eyes never leaving hers, as he unbuckled his pants and pushed them to the floor. She sucked in a breath at the sight of him standing at the foot of the bed, handsome, hard, and obviously ready for her. He snapped his fingers and turned away, finding his bag and rummaging through until he produced a small foil packet. He shook the packet playfully before joining her on the bed, crawling on top of her.

Heat radiated from his body as he lowered himself onto her, his erection practically pulsing against her. They kissed, deep and searching, as his teasing hands roamed over her body. Her hips swiveled up to meet him, only her panties separating them, and he pushed against her. He trailed kisses all over her body, leaving her wanting more of him, all of him, until he sat up and rocked back on his heels. He hooked his fingers through the sides of her panties and pulled them off in one swift motion before flinging them behind him. His knees pushed her legs apart, and he settled in between them.

"You're so beautiful, Carly. I've always wanted you, wanted this. I can't wait another minute." At his words, she was afraid she would explode before he even touched her. He rolled the condom on and flashed her a look, her crazy lust for him reflected in his own eyes.

"Me neither." She managed to say the words, then he was on her, crushing her lips in a searing kiss.

He ran his hands over her body until they reached the apex of her thighs. Michael slowed down and explored her gently with a soft caress. She pushed her hips up to meet his touch, encouraging him, and he moved to suck her earlobe into his mouth, nipping gently.

"Last chance. Are you sure you want this?" His voice was husky, his breath hot against her skin. "That you want me?"

"Oh, yes." She groaned. She was past wanting him. Now she needed him, and she was so tired of fighting it.

Needing no further encouragement, he entered her, and she arched her back to meet him. They stayed joined and motionless for the briefest moment. They were perfectly matched, as she knew they would be, fitting together as effortlessly as they had that morning. As he moved within her, she pulled him close to her, her hands splayed across back and shoulders. His enchanting, warm scent drifted over her, their ragged breath intermingling. The haze of lust clouding her mind allowed her to forget that this wasn't real. Just for the moment, she let herself believe that this was more than physical attraction. He filled her, completely and exquisitely, and everything was perfect.

"You're so beautiful. So sexy." Her eyelids fluttered closed as his words washed over her, pushing her to new heights of pleasure. Never in her wildest fantasies had she imagined that Michael Welch would turn her on so completely, that he'd know just what to do and say. "You feel so good." Her climax crashed through her as she hooked her ankles behind his back and pulled him closer.

Michael held her hips as he drove into her, deeper and harder, until he stiffened with his own climax. He collapsed on top of her, covering her with his delicious weight, motionless while their breathing slowed. He pulled out of her and fell to her side, encircling her in his arms. She snuggled into his embrace, enjoying the contentment that washed over her. She found the nook between his neck and collarbone and nestled in, finding that it felt more like home than anything ever had before. Her lips brushed the soft skin of his neck, and she settled into his embrace with an arm resting at his hip.

His fingertips ran over her curves lazily, and they lay together silently in the afterglow. His breath was warm against her as he kissed the top of her head. Tomorrow, she'd deal with the cold hard facts. Tonight, she would sleep in the arms of her perfect man, completely satisfied.

• • •

Michael skimmed his hand over Carly's hips and settled on the peachy curve of her butt, unable to resist giving her a little squeeze. The soft glow of the bedside alarm clock illuminated her with a subtle light. She was just right, the perfect shape and size to fit against him.

When they'd woken up that morning, tangled up in one another, he'd held his breath, afraid that she would realize she'd worked her way into his arms. He knew the moment she fully awoke, since her body stiffened immediately. She seemed so mortified to be tucked against him that he pretended to be asleep. For the few moments he had her there, secure and content beside him, before she woke and moved away, he could pretend that she returned his growing feelings, that they were as good a pair as he thought.

After that sweet night, he never thought they'd actually take things as far as they did. As her breathing became more regular, a soft sigh escaped her lips and landed straight in his chest. If only she was always like this, always happy in his arms. Michael's last real relationship, so long ago, had almost convinced himself he didn't want another one. He didn't, not really, until Carly came into his life. But a woman like her wouldn't want a relationship with him. He was a joke to her, beneath her, and the only way he'd ever worked his way into her good graces was because he'd taken her out of her element. That was all it was.

Once they returned home, she'd remember she couldn't stand to be in the same room with him. The glimpses of attraction in her eyes had been just that—attraction, and nothing more. The relationship charade and crazy scrutiny of the show had brought out her insecurities, and she needed him to hold on to. There was nothing more between them, and he had to remember that before he did something stupid. No real feelings were behind her heated gazes. Once they were back home, she'd shut down; he was sure of it.

Harsh reality could wait, though, and tonight, he'd enjoy the perfect fit of the most amazing woman he'd ever met. He pulled her close, breathing in her intoxicating fragrance, and whispered in her ear, "I wish you could really be mine."

She sighed and snuggled closer before mumbling, "Me, too."

Chapter Nine

Carly held Michael's note, roughly scrawled on hotel stationary, in trembling fingers. Disappointment sat in her stomach like a rock, weighing down the bubbly happiness that carried her off to sleep the night before. What had she expected would happen? That she'd wake up in his arms and somehow their relationship would be real? That one night together was magical enough to change him? She should've known better. If she expected him to respect her feelings, it would have been necessary to actually share them with him. And she wasn't going there. Her decision to keep work and romance separate was a good one. Nothing had changed, and the sooner she got that through her head, the better.

She sat up, still tangled in the sheets. His scent lingered in the air, that complex bergamot and leather combination, and longing gripped her. Michael, whose every word and action worked her last nerve, had somehow managed to wind his way under her skin.

But he apparently had no trouble hopping out of bed and getting on with his day. She would do well to follow his lead. He wouldn't come back to their room to find her vulnerable and needy, still lying in bed, waiting for him. She'd be showered, dressed, and neatly made up.

Her phone buzzed on the dresser, pulling her thoughts back to the present. She checked the display, and seeing that her mother was on the line, decided not to answer. It was too soon to hold a normal conversation, and the last thing she needed was a reminder of her horrible taste in men. Her parents encouraged her to find a suitable guy to settle down with, but as usual, she'd gone for the guy who'd leave her feeling needy and used. A pad of hotel stationary caught her eye, and she scanned the notes scratched across the page. Michael had doodled along the edges, but had jotted down information, probably during a phone call. He'd written the name "Kelly," an address, and something else he'd scratched out. So that explained his "something" that came up.

Bile rose in her throat as the reality of her situation washed over her. To her, their night together had been a revelation, an awakening. She'd never felt so connected to a man before, and it wasn't just him; it was the way they were together. Last night wasn't supposed to mean anything, but it did, and she had no one to blame but herself. To him, it was obviously just a night of sex, nothing more, and he was off to meet another woman before the sheets were cold. She'd learned a little about Michael during their trip, but nothing had changed. Beneath it all, he was the same guy he'd always been, and she was the sucker who'd let her heart get away from her.

. . .

Michael came back to a silent hotel room, head buzzing with possibilities and eager to see Carly again. Her suitcase sat on top of the neatly made bed, but she was nowhere to be found. He'd woken that morning to find her sleeping deeply, long sooty lashes dark against her creamy skin. Her auburn hair fanned across the pillow, beckoning his fingers to touch the silky strands. When she'd moaned in her sleep and flipped over onto her stomach, he'd almost crawled back under the covers. It would have been so easy to slip in beside her and let his hands roam over her curves, to gently wake her with his touch. What he wouldn't give to have her just once more ...

But they hadn't discussed anything further than last night, her gorgeous ass notwithstanding. Leaving her lying in bed that morning was near impossible, but he couldn't say no when his former agent texted him, wanting to meet while he was in town.

The door lock clicked, and Carly came in. She was polished and buttoned-up, her hair pulled into a low ponytail and her skin covered by her conservative blouse and skirt. Like a sexy librarian, one who might shush you and punish you for disobeying. He grinned at the thought of her delivering a spanking, but stopped when their eyes met. One look at her face told him the wild woman who'd spent a night of reckless abandon in his arms was long gone. The Carly he'd known before was back, walls between them firmly erected, protective armor locked in place.

"Hey," he said, unable to keep the smile from returning to his face. She might want nothing to do with him, but he'd never let that stop him before. "Sorry I slipped out this morning without telling you. You looked so beautiful lying there that I didn't want to wake you. Did you see my note?"

"Yes, I got your note." She bit out the words, clearly unmoved. The ice princess was back in full force. Obviously nothing, not even the heat that burned between them the night before, could melt her chilly poise.

He had to laugh. She was just too much, acting like this after what they shared. Hadn't she felt what he did? Hadn't it affected her? "All right then, I see how things are. Do you want to grab some lunch before our flight? Or are we done now that you've had your taste?"

A furious blush colored her cheeks. "What? No. Had my taste? What do you even mean?"

"We still have the room for a few more hours, if you want a repeat of last night. I'm game if you are." He shouldn't tease her, but she was so cute when flustered. Besides, there was always the slight chance that she'd say yes, and Michael wasn't about to say no to another round between the sheets with Carly.

"I should've known that you'd act like this." The fire was gone. She sounded resigned and disappointed, not irritated like usual.

His heart sank. Over the past few days, they'd made so much progress. He thought she had seen past the surface to find she could respect and depend on him, but now it was as though nothing had changed.

"Hey, I'm sorry, cupcake." He closed the distance and ran his hands up and down her arms. "I was teasing you, and I shouldn't. Forgive me?"

He gave her his most charming smile, and a look of surrender flashed in her eyes, gone as quickly as it had come. A second later, she was composed, back to her normal self. "Of course. It's fine. There's nothing to forgive."

Up close, she smelled fresh, like grapefruit and flowers, nothing like her usual cozy vanilla fragrance. It was delicious, but he missed the sweet scent he'd always associated with her. "How about lunch, then? I mean, you've got to eat, don't you? Let's grab a bite before we head out."

The tension left her arms, but she slipped out of his grasp. "Sure, sounds great."

She avoided eye contact as she crossed the room to grab her handbag. Their relationship was nothing more than a charade, he knew that, but why couldn't she see that underneath the animosity there might be something real and wonderful? Great sex was one thing; what they'd shared was on a whole other level. Maybe he'd enjoyed it more than she had—though if that were the case, she was one hell of an actress. She'd convinced the cameras that she was his girlfriend, so he could've underestimated her, but he didn't think so. As they walked down the empty hallway toward the elevator, he let his hand land at the small of her back, briefly enjoying how perfectly they fit together before pulling back.

•••

They took their seats in the crowded Italian restaurant recommended by the hotel concierge, and Carly moved the Chianti bottle doubling as a candleholder so she could enjoy the view for a moment as Michael bent his head over to study the menu. The pendant light hung low over their table, bringing out the golden flecks in his eyes. Everything was so confusing now. She was such an idiot. To think she'd actually felt something for him, started to let herself rely on him. It was a blessing that she'd seen the notepad and hadn't risked spilling her guts. They'd defined the parameters of their relationship clearly, but of course she'd let herself get carried away.

He looked up when their waitress approached, flashing the pretty brunette the charming smile he used on every woman. They placed their orders, and she gave them each a tall glass of ice water before leaving them alone. Without the waitress or menus to distract them, they were forced to face each other, and the silence stretched out in a thick, garlicky haze. At least he'd finally stopped looking like he didn't think anything was wrong. Michael flipped a sugar packet back and forth on the table before finally taking a deep breath and looking her in the eye, sending her heart rate off at a swift gallop.

"So, I guess there's no use in beating around the bush. I've got something to tell you." He kept his eyes trained on the Chianti bottle with its waxy rivulets running down its sides, avoiding hers.

Carly held her breath, hoping despite herself, despite all signs to the contrary, that he would say he had feelings for her. She swallowed, and arranged her features in what she hoped was a neutral, open expression. "Sure, what is it?"

He scrubbed a hand over his face and waited for what felt like an eternity before looking up again. "Ah, there's no easy way to say this, but a big opportunity has come up, and I don't know what to do."

She held her breath for a second, switching gears and letting his words sink in. His nervousness had nothing to do with her or what they'd shared the night before. There would be no exploration of feelings, no fumbling declaration of affection. "What do you mean?"

"You know how I was gone this morning?" Of course, how could she forget? "I had an impromptu meeting with my old agent. She texted me last night, and I must have missed it. I didn't have a chance to tell you, and I didn't want to wake you this morning. Since we're making the appearance on *Sugar Shock*, she pitched me for a new show that the network is considering, and it looks like I have another shot at shooting a pilot. If I want it."

"Wow, that's the last thing I expected to hear." She'd been so convinced that he blew her off for another woman that she never considered that maybe her feelings were reciprocated, that the magic between them was real. Despite herself, hope welled up in her chest.

"I'm pretty surprised myself. I thought our appearance on the show would be a one-and-done kind of thing, and I never thought it would lead to anything else. I've learned so much since the first time around, though, that it might not be a bad idea. This new show could actually work out—you know, if I don't mess it up again."

"Wow. Congratulations. That's great news. What about your sister?"

"Our aunt can visit her while I'm here. I'd try to get home as often as possible while we're getting started, and after that, it sounds like the kind of show that will shoot on location. I'll be away from her more than I would like, but I won't have to move here or anything."

"I guess it's perfect, then. Having your own show is what you've always wanted, right? Sounds like an amazing opportunity." What else could she say? His life was about to have a whole lot less to do with her than ever.

"It is, but it could complicate things." He traced the condensation on the outside of his glass. "For you."

"What does it have to do with me?" Besides the fact that she let herself fall for him, and now nothing could happen.

"I'd have to stay here and get to work right away. It would leave you high and dry for the Grainger-Rivers wedding."

Oh, that. Yet another glaring example of Michael's undependable nature. Tears prickled behind her eyes, but she wouldn't allow herself to get emotional. He was clearly ready to move on, and she wouldn't stop him. "I'm pretty sure I can handle it on my own. I'll get another baker to assist if I need help. Don't worry about me." Although she couldn't do relationships or casual sex, Carly could handle a wedding cake.

"I haven't said yes yet. I could always turn it down and stay where I am, just go back home and keep working at my shop. Nothing has to change. If you want me to stay, I'll stay. Just say the word." His green eyes were hopeful, searching. Was he hoping for her blessing? He wanted her to dismiss him so he could leave without guilt.

She did want him to stay with her, more than anything. But he wasn't talking about exploring their feelings, or whether the magic of their one night together could go further. He was talking about the job, nothing more. It was as though their experiences had been completely different. She'd let herself believe that the way they fit together perfectly meant something. It didn't. It meant that they had chemistry, not that her feelings were real. It didn't mean that she could count on him.

"I've done hundreds of weddings, many of them without any help. If you want to get another show started, I won't stand in your way. You should do what you want to do." Surely he didn't think that she needed him badly enough that she'd ask him to give up his dream.

"Okay, great. I'm sure you're right, and it'll be fine. You'll do great on your own." He flashed her a bright smile, but it didn't reach his eyes.

• • •

Michael shoved his socks into his suitcase and yanked the zipper closed. He should have known better than to think that Carly would ask him to stay with her, that she felt something for him. When Carly had asked about his sister, a light bulb had gone on. Nobody ever asked him about Jenny, or acknowledged that he was important to her. Carly got it. She understood, and thought about Jenny's care almost as quickly as he would have. Nobody had ever done that before. But instead of all the pieces falling into place, they were packing up to head their separate ways.

He should've known better, should've taken things slower. He'd pounced on her when she was vulnerable and had used the situation to his advantage. She'd been forced to pretend she liked him, that being close to him was a pleasure rather than a chore. She'd let down her guard and got caught up in the moment, but that was it. Did he really think that giving her an ultimatum would force her hand, would make her admit to having some feelings for him?

Carly joined him, turning her wrist to check her watch. She was the only person he knew who still wore a watch instead of checking her cell phone for the time. He'd miss that. He'd miss her. Damn, he was getting sappy.

"They're sending someone to take us to the airport, right? Or should I call a cab?"

"I think one of the production assistants will pick us up. You packed and ready to roll?" He tried for an easy tone, as if his hopes hadn't just been shot down. She didn't try to convince him to reconsider, of course. She was ready to get back to normal, and he would oblige her. If she wanted things to change, she would've said so when he laid it all out for her. He was a grade-A idiot for thinking that one night together could change her mind about him.

"Yep. I'm ready when you are." Her words were light. Was there the slightest hint of longing? No, he was probably imagining things, projecting his own desires onto her.

"All right then, let's head out." The sooner they got out of this hotel, the sooner he'd be out of her life and moving on.

Michael dropped his suitcase to the floor and pulled the handle out. When she moved her hair off her shoulder to loop her carry-on bag over her arm, a puff of uniquely Carly-scented air stopped him in his tracks. This was ridiculous. She didn't want him, didn't even flinch when he said he was leaving. This was only a job to her, no matter how much he wanted it to mean something more.

Chapter Ten

Sequoia Rivers slipped into Caketopia through the back entrance, her slight frame dwarfed by her floppy hat, oversized sunglasses, and huge full-length coat. Her signature sunshine-blonde hair was tucked under her hat. Carly had to smile at the lengths the young celebrity went to in order to protect her anonymity. Since announcing her engagement to Rusty Grainger, the paparazzi had dogged her more than ever. Any moment she could get without a camera in her face was probably like a breath of fresh air.

Sequoia shot a furtive glance over her shoulder. "I don't think I was followed, but you can never be too careful. They're everywhere, and they never stop."

Carly led her down the hallway toward her workroom. "We'll be safe here. Layla won't let anyone past the storefront."

Sequoia grinned at her, wrinkling her slim nose. "I'm sure that big strong boyfriend of yours keeps this place pretty safe. Where is Michael?"

Oh, him. "He's out of town. Can I get you something to drink before we get started? Coffee, water, soda?" The less she thought about Michael, the better.

Sequoia shrugged out of the coat and shook her hair out of the hat. "No, thanks, I had some delicious kombucha before I came over. In fact, I'll bring some by for you next time we meet. You'll love it, and it'll keep you healthy for the big day."

Carly was careful not to wrinkle her nose as she pasted a bright smile on her face. She didn't know what kombucha was, but it sounded smelly. "That would be great, thanks."

Carly pulled the big lavender binder dedicated to the Grainger-Rivers wedding from her shelf and set it in front of the actress. "I'm glad you came in today. With your wedding day so close, we need to finalize your choices." She flipped the binder open and turned the pages. "So, here we have three designs to choose from, based on what we discussed in our emails. At this point, we can still go back and pick one from earlier, but sometimes it's easier to look at a smaller pool of potential cakes."

Sequoia's mossy-green eyes narrowed in concentration, her delicate brow furrowed. "Hmm. I do still like these three the best." She flipped back and forth between the cake sketches.

"Any of them speak to you more than the others?" Carly was surprised Sequoia didn't have some kind of spiritual advisor for this choice. The ghost of a smile tugged at her lips, the first since she and Michael had parted ways, as she pictured Sequoia hanging a crystal over the binder to receive divine wisdom.

"I really like this one. I keep coming back to it, and it's what I would've drawn," she said with a laugh. "You know, if I could actually draw."

Sequoia had chosen Carly's personal favorite, and her initial stirrings of excitement over the wedding returned. The prospect of designing a cake that could put her on the map had made her head spin with possibilities when they began this adventure, and it was nice to have something to look forward to again. Michael stealing her heart and leaving it in Los Angeles had squashed most of the joy she'd gotten from revving up her creative engine. The new work that would surely come her way afterwards would surely be enough to keep her mind off Michael.

"Do you think the wedding cake and groom's cake should match? I don't know if I want them to be totally different." Sequoia twisted her lips to one side in concentration. "It feels like it could be unbalanced if we don't do something similar."

"Honestly, it doesn't matter if they are the same or completely opposite. We'll have them on different tables, at least, and we can even place them in different areas at the reception location. We can certainly make sure that the two are complementary, though, if that concerns you."

"I do feel like they should complement one another, but I told Rusty he could choose whatever he wanted. I'm sure he and Michael are cooking up something wild that I'll hate." The look of love in her eyes when she talked about Rusty pulled at Carly's heart. She'd never have that for herself if she spent all her time mooning over Michael Welch and their failed fake relationship.

"Actually, I'm doing the groom's cake as well. Michael is going to be caught up in Los Angeles for the next several months. Did he not tell Rusty?" She hated delivering bad news, especially to someone as flighty as Sequoia.

"No, he didn't say a word. What's going on? Rusty loves Michael's work." Sequoia sat up straight on the stool. The carefree attitude was gone, along with the dreamy look in her eyes.

Carly twisted her hands together. "I'm so sorry, because I thought he'd already told you about this. Michael got an offer to stay in L.A. and shoot a television pilot, so he won't be here. Don't worry, though, because I can absolutely handle both cakes with no problem. This is the biggest wedding I've ever done, but I'm confident that I can deliver everything we've promised. I have the staff I need to assist, and it'll be great with or without him. Michael gave me the designs he worked up for the groom's cake, so we can do whatever Rusty chooses." Carly hoped her professional confidence would reassure Sequoia, but the light hadn't returned to her eyes.

"I don't think he'll go for that, honey. He was really excited about working with Michael himself. What kind of pilot is he shooting? What happened?"

"You know that we were contestants on that show *Sugar Shock*, right?" Sequoia nodded. "Well, once word got out that we were doing the cakes for your wedding, the producers invited us out to shoot a segment in L.A. for their Valentine's Day episode. Michael ended up meeting with his old agent when we were in town. He's always wanted his own show, and when he got a chance to do another cake show, he just couldn't pass it up." Carly shrugged. The truth was painful, but the sooner she faced it, the sooner she could move on.

"So, just like that, he's gone? That must be strange to go from working together and seeing each other all the time to having a long-distance relationship. What are you two going to do?" Sequoia propped her elbows on the steel table, eyes full of sympathy.

The genuine concern on Sequoia's face made Carly sorry they'd ever started the stupid charade. Having her own feelings stomped all over was one thing, but to make someone else feel for her imaginary breakup was another. "We decided it would be best to break up."

"What? You two are perfect for each other!" Sequoia sat up straight again, genuine surprise on her delicate features.

They really were perfect together, weren't they? Carly could deny it all she wanted, but she had fallen for Michael. She loved his confidence and effortless style. He always made her feel like she could lean on him, stepping into the role as though it were made for him. Once she dropped her determination to hate everything about him, Carly could recognize his talent and skill, combined with a fearless flair that nobody could replicate. Their chemistry had to be real; she didn't imagine that. But just because they seemed custom-made for one another didn't mean that they were really meant to be together. The fact that he was gorgeous and amazing in bed just made it harder to admit that she'd created a relationship in her head. It was so like her to find meaning where there was none.

"I guess he didn't think so, or at least not perfect enough for him to give up on following his dream." Carly shrugged.

"Wait, are you saying he broke up with you?" Sequoia's eyes were wide with disbelief.

"Yeah, pretty much. I wouldn't make him choose between staying with me and following his dream, but I guess he did anyway." He was the one who'd left, after all.

Sequoia grimaced, sucking in air through her teeth. "I'm sorry, honey, but I'm worried about the cakes now. Maybe I should find someone else."

Carly straightened. "Honestly, Sequoia, I can handle it on my own. I've done hundreds of weddings, and I have ample staff to help out and make sure it all goes off without a hitch."

Sequoia laid a hand on Carly's arm. "I know that you could make a cake without Michael, but this changes things. Your sorrow and heartbreak will make its way into the cakes, and it's bad for the energy of our wedding. We went with you and Michael specifically because the food that represents our union needs to be infused with loving energy. I just can't take the chance that your tears will end up in the cake batter. I love your designs, though, so I'd like to figure out a way to keep you on the job without compromising the purity of the work."

Great. Not only had she lost the man she could have fallen in love with, she now she might lose the biggest job of her career, too. Gone, everything, just like that. And all because she couldn't bring herself to ask him to stay. He might have shot her down, but he might have returned her feelings. She'd never know now, and they'd never have the chance. All because she was afraid. Afraid that she wasn't what he wanted, afraid to admit her feelings, afraid to take a chance for once and trust her feelings with a man.

Brokenhearted or not, she was a professional to her core. "I'm certainly disappointed, but the baker you work with is a personal choice. I certainly hope you decide that we can still work together, but I'll understand if you don't."

"I hope we can still work together, too, Carly. I'll do my best to figure out how to make that happen."

Carly walked Sequoia out of the workroom, holding her head high and her tears at bay. Summoning her last reserve of calm professionalism, she gave Sequoia her best wishes for a happy wedding day and turned on her heel to rush back to her workroom. Tears fell before the door closed behind her, and she crumpled onto her chair, miserable.

•••

Michael shifted in the hard plastic chair, trying to get comfortable across from Kelly McCall's clear Lucite desk. His agent's office was modern, everything white or clear, all clean lines and hard surfaces. Things had changed since the first time they'd worked together, when she shared a shabby office space with a guy who represented animal actors. Kelly held up one perfectly manicured finger to indicate that she'd be off her phone call soon, and Michael hooked his ankle over his knee. Oversized prints lined her wall, each looking like blobs that his six-year-old cousin could've painted, but probably costing more than his first car. The sleek espresso machine and individual glass bottles of water in the corner suggested that she was making a lot more money than before, and that her client list had grown. All Kelly used to serve was scorched coffee and tepid generic soda with cat hair clinging to the can.

"All right, hon. Call me later to let me know how it went. I'll be thinking of you, keeping my fingers crossed. Good luck." She paused, listening, and rolled her eyes. "All right, bye bye, now."

She ended her call and leaned forward on her elbows. "Thanks for coming in, Michael. It's awesome to see you again."

He sat up straight. "You too, Kelly. I'm excited to get back to work."

She shuffled a stack of folders on her desk and turned to her computer screen. As she jiggled her mouse, she narrowed her eyes in concentration. "All right, here we are." She scribbled on an index card. "Here's the name of the guy at Cuisine Network you need to meet with, hon. I sent the contract over to legal, but it looks pretty boilerplate. I'll have more information for you if they find anything. In the meantime, the Cuisine Network suits will talk you through their concept, and you'll have a chance to ask questions or offer input."

He picked up the index card and read the address. "Just like that?"

"Yeah, just like that." She smiled, clearly pleased to have made a deal so quickly.

"Wow." He shifted in the chair, running his hands down his thighs. "Great, then. I guess I'll get over there."

"Sounds great. Just remember, they're pumped up about the new show and seem to be excited to welcome you back, but it can all change. Until you sign on the dotted line, be sure to watch what you say and do. We want to make a good impression; you never know when these guys will decide they aren't so interested after all." Her eyes were already scanning her cell phone; she was clearly finished with their meeting.

He stood, feeling deflated though he knew she was only being cautious. He might be overeager, probably a little cocky, but he wasn't stupid. He wouldn't go in acting like a superstar, and his agent didn't need to remind him how to act professionally.

"All right, thanks, Kelly. Let me know when you get the contract, and I'll come back in."

"Sure thing. And Michael, don't forget: they came to us, not the other way around. They already love you. Don't worry about a thing." She gave him a brilliant, showbiz smile, revealing a fleck of bright red lipstick stuck to her tooth.

Mustering enthusiasm for the meeting, he left. Losing Carly had put a damper on the excitement he should be feeling about getting the second chance of a lifetime. He'd been dumped before, of course, but had never been so devastated by losing someone. She wasn't even really his, which made it that much more confusing. Surely she knew that he was asking if she wanted to be with him when he offered to stay. Didn't she? If he weren't such a coward, he would've confessed that his feelings for her were real and asked if she felt the same. Whatever she said, at least he'd know one way or the other. Now it was too late, and he had to accept that.

• • •

Michael sat in a generic room with a few dozen guys who looked just like him. A Cuisine Network staffer in a tailored suit burst through the door and made a beeline toward his seat, arm outstretched for a handshake.

"Michael Welch, it's so nice to meet you. I'm Timothy King." Michael stood and took the man's hand. "They should have sent you back to me directly. I guess there was some kind of misunderstanding. I hope you weren't waiting long."

"No, in fact, I've only been here about five minutes." Michael ignored the curious stares of the other men in the room. Auditioning, going out on calls, vying for the same job as twenty other dudes—it was a relief to have grown out of the desperate auditioning phase. After being out of the game so long, he wasn't sure he could do it again. The other guys had to resent him, hate that he'd been plucked out of the crowd without even having to sing and dance.

"Come with me, and we'll get you started." Timothy was on his way back to the door without another word, clearly expecting Michael to follow along and keep up.

They strode through the hallways of Cuisine Network's business offices, past framed posters from current and former programs, until they reached a conference room. Timothy opened the door and let Michael walk in ahead of him. Five executives sat around a chrome and glass table, tapping on their cell phones.

"Gentlemen, this is Michael Welch. He was in the waiting room this whole time." Timothy announced to the group. "They had him sitting with the actors auditioning for *Soup's On*." The group laughed, and Timothy led him to a seat. Michael took the empty chair and tried for an expression that said "calm and confident, but not too confident."

"Michael, this is Greg Fields. He's the one who came up with the brilliant idea to track down your agent and see about getting you back on the network," Timothy introduced an executive wearing a tailored suit with a scarlet tie.

Greg shook hands with Michael, then filled his water glass and began the meeting. "Michael, we reviewed the film from *Sugar Shock*'s Valentine's Day episode and were reminded of how much we at Cuisine Network enjoy you. We originally thought about pulling you in for some guest hosting spots, but after talking with your agent, we knew that you needed your own vehicle. You're too talented and charismatic to waste on guest appearances. So here's what we're thinking." He paused to take a drink of water. "*Around the World in Thirteen Cakes* with Michael Welch."

He propped a mock-up of the show's poster on a small easel. "We'll start with the pilot, and if it flies, we think the network will buy thirteen episodes. Fewer or more, and we can change the title if we need to, like *Around the World in Twenty Cakes* or whatever. Here's the concept. Think Cuisine Network meets Vacation Channel. Each episode will feature a unique vacation destination, where you'll explore the local culture and tourist attractions, maybe with a special focus on cuisine, and a unique cake to reflect the visit. It can be either a design specific to the destination, depicting a landmark, or something that viewers will understand after watching your footage. What do you think?"

Michael shifted in his chair. "I think it sounds amazing, and I'd be thrilled to work on a show like that. Thank you for thinking of me." It was happening incredibly fast, and he wasn't sure he could fit in the specific mold the network set for him, but he'd keep that under his hat. Half his success could be attributed to faking it when he wasn't sure he was up to the task, and this show would be no exception.

Chapter Eleven

Carly looked around the near-empty department store as Lily flipped through a rack of dresses, hangers clanging against the rod. Her trained eyes scanned each piece at warp speed, able to assess and reject a dress within seconds. Lily knew fashion, and she knew what looked best on her, something Carly had been trying to pick up from her best friend for years. Lily was attending a fundraiser dinner with a congressman she'd been seeing, and she was looking for something that would show off her best features but be conservative enough to pass muster amid the political heavy hitters that would be in attendance.

"So, if you do this sage smear," Lily wrinkled her nose, "you'll be cleared of enough negative energy for her to let you make the wedding cake again?"

"It's a sage smudge, and yes. I'll only be clear enough to bake her cake if I complete the smudge; otherwise, I think she'll take me off the job. It seemed like she was really close to doing just that when I told her that Michael left. I feel lucky, but it wouldn't surprise me one bit if she asks me to do some other weird detox routine after this." Carly dug around in her purse until she found a tin of mints and popped one in her mouth. Offering the tin to Lily, she continued. "Sequoia Rivers personally smudged my workroom at Caketopia and even did a special session on me."

"She wiped sage on you?"

"No, of course not! You light the smudge stick and blow it out to let it smolder, like an incense stick, which she also sent me home with a healthy supply of. You can't touch it or rub it directly on anything, because, you know, it's smoldering hot. You just take the stick and wave it throughout the space, or in my case, around my body, with purpose. The smoke clears the negative energy that has accumulated."

"With purpose? Like with love and light and positive intentions?" Lily cocked an eyebrow. She was open-minded and well-traveled, but she clearly thought the sage smudge cleanse was ridiculous.

Carly had to giggle. When Sequoia had explained the process, she was dead serious, but hearing the words repeated by Lily made it sound like such a joke. "Yeah, she gave me a clearing kit for my apartment and told me to cleanse the whole place several times a year. She said that even homes with the best feng shui have negative energy accumulate. I think it's cute that she thinks I've even considered my apartment's feng shui." She pulled a royal-blue dress from the rack. "How about this one?"

Lily touched the slinky fabric. "It's pretty, but he's a Republican. I shouldn't wear blue. I need to try to find something in red."

Carly put the dress back on the rack and ran her fingertips over the tops of the hangers. "Did you watch the episode?" she asked without making eye contact. The *Sugar Shock* Valentine's Day episode had aired, but Carly had been too chicken to watch it. Besides, she was already exhausted. Caketopia always did brisk business around the romantic holiday, so she'd taken on all the work she'd normally delegate to keep her mind off things. She hadn't seen Michael in several weeks, but the pain was as fresh as the day she came home from filming.

Lily laid a gentle hand on her arm. "I did, and it was really good. I think you should watch it. You're torturing yourself, wondering what it's like and reliving every moment. Just put yourself out of your misery and get it over with. It's probably way less painful than you're imagining, but I can watch it with you. We can hang at my place if you want. I'll order takeout and pick up extra bottles of wine to fortify you." She rubbed her hand up and down Carly's arm. "Sound good?"

Carly nodded, still not sure she could look into the sympathetic eyes of her friend. Besides being able to practically read her mind and see right through her assurances that everything was fine, Lily's eyes were more expressive than most. They had won her more than a few choice modeling contracts, and looking into them when you were sad was like asking for the tears to start falling.

Carly couldn't pretend that her heart wasn't broken any longer. She hadn't been able to bring herself to admit out loud that she had fallen for Michael or that losing him was harder than she ever would've imagined, but she didn't have to say it. Lily knew her well enough to see that there was more to it than just the job, and that she'd spill her secrets in her own time.

"That sounds good. Might as well get it over with, and it'll be easier with a friend by my side." Carly offered her a weak smile. "Now, is there anything in this store you can wear to this event, or are we done here?"

•••

Carly settled into Lily's plush burgundy sofa, marveling as always at her friend's impeccable taste. Years of working in the fashion industry and traveling around the world had influenced Lily's style in a way that put Carly's catalogue-curated apartment décor to shame. Lily effortlessly blended colors, textures, and styles in ways that created a home that was welcoming and intriguing. Every time Carly visited, she wanted to nest in the rich fabrics of her chairs and blankets or spend hours flipping through her thick leather-bound books. Lily managed to make her apartment feel like an international vacation without the culture shock.

"Cute. Are these new?" Carly pushed two miniature golden elephants across the end table.

Lily handed Carly a hand-blown balloon goblet of lush ruby pinot noir and settled onto the couch beside her. Takeout boxes and black stoneware dinner plates littered the marble coffee table in front of them. "They were a gift from the congressman. Told you he was a Republican."

"He must like you, taking you to fancy high-profile dinners, giving you gifts." Carly trailed off and sipped her wine.

Lily tucked her feet beneath her and snuggled into the sofa. "Nah, he just needs someone to smile pretty for the photographers. When we're alone, he barely talks about anything beyond his schedule and his platform. I'm pretty sure he thinks I wouldn't understand the issues he's involved with." She grabbed the remote control and turned the television on. As she flipped through her recorded shows to find *Sugar Shock*, she leaned forward and speared a chunk of orange chicken straight from the box. "And that's fine by me. I'm not interested in sharing my life story with him just yet."

Carly spooned garlic noodles and spicy shrimp onto her plate and settled in to eat dinner while they watched. The familiar *Sugar Shock* theme music and opening scenes filled the screen, and before she and Michael even showed up, Carly's heart began to race. Shelley Peabody's flawless face smiled at the camera and told the viewers they were in for a special treat. She recapped the competition as scenes from the current season's episodes flashed by in a montage, offered her sincere well wishes for the contestant who'd been sent home the week before, and hinted that the viewers were in for a big surprise. Commercials flew by as Lily fast-forwarded, and Carly slurped a garlicky noodle through her lips. After seeing the difference between what actually happened on set and the editors' finished product, she was more than a little nervous to see how she and Michael would be portrayed.

Lily stopped when the *Sugar Shock* logo flashed back on the screen, and Carly held her breath, knowing that they were surely up next. Shelley welcomed the audience back to the show and took them on a trip down memory lane, reminding viewers of season-three contestants Carly and Michael and their volatile relationship.

They included the infamous scene where she'd thrown the bag full of bright blue buttercream at Michael, and she had to laugh as it splattered across his otherwise pristine chef's whites. Clips from their original season confessional interviews aired, and Carly was horrified to see how nasty and hateful she came off when she was asked about Michael, especially compared to how he laughed about their rivalry. She cringed at footage of her sneering into the camera, deriding Michael's success and calling him "a ridiculous excuse for a man." She looked away from the screen as a scene showed her rolling her eyes at something Michael said during the competition.

Seeing it now, it was no surprise that she'd been sent home. He was professional while she was emotional, and her behavior was appalling. It was no wonder he could let her go so easily. She'd never given him a reason to think that she'd be a good bet, had always focused on dragging him down.

The interview between the two of them began, and Lily turned to her, brown eyes wide, smile even wider. "You like him! I thought I saw something between you two the first time I watched the episode. Now I'm certain."

"What? Don't be ridiculous!" Carly sipped her wine, a telltale blush creeping into her pale cheeks.

"Look at that body language. You're practically curled into him like a cat. And he clearly has it bad for you, sister. I love the way he looks at you, like a man in love." She sighed and put a hand over her heart. "It's so romantic."

"It's an act, all for the camera. He's an old pro, remember? Trust me, Michael Welch is not a man in love. Not with me at least."

They cut to scenes spliced from their cooking lesson, and even Carly felt her breath catch when she saw the two of them together. They danced like two lovers who couldn't get enough of one another, as though no matter how close they got, it would never be close enough. Michael's eyes burned with passion as he looked down at her during their impromptu dance, and she looked as though she might melt into him. Together, they looked like they actually knew what they were doing. He was confident enough to lead, and she was brave enough to trust him.

"How can you not see it? You two were made for one another. I can't believe you let him get away. I just can't." Lily threw up her hands. "I don't know what I'm going to do with you, girl."

"He left. I didn't let him get away." She couldn't deny it any longer. She had fallen for Michael, and now he was gone.

Scenes from their time at the microbrewery flashed by in a blur as tears filled Carly's eyes. They sat side by side at the bar, heads inclined as they ate, and he dipped a French fry in ketchup before feeding it to her. He followed it with a sweet kiss, and her heart broke as she watched him tilt her chin up to meet his lips before whispering in her ear.

Had she known how much she would crave his touch when he was gone, she would've memorized every moment they had together. Lily scooted toward her and pulled her into her arms, rubbing her back in gentle circles. "Aw, honey, I was teasing you. I'm sorry. You really miss him, don't you?"

She couldn't answer, but nodded and sniffled loudly. Hot tears rolled down her cheeks, landing in fat puddles on her jeans as she pulled away from her friend. "I don't know how it happened, but somehow I fell for him." It hurt, but it was a relief to finally say it out loud.

Lily patted her hand. "From the looks of it, he fell for you, too. Why didn't you ask him to stay?"

She took a deep, shuddering breath and swiped the tears from her cheeks with the back of her hand. "All he ever really wanted was to have his own show. He said he would stay if I wanted him to, that he would turn down the pilot, but I wasn't about to ask him to give that up for me."

"Wait, he actually said that he would stay with you if you wanted? Does he know how you feel about him?"

"Of course not. I didn't even admit it to myself until now. I couldn't ask him to give up the chance to have his own show, not for me at least. I'm not the type of woman he goes for, and the last thing I wanted was for him to have to let me down easy."

"You are ridiculous, Carly Piper. You're beautiful, smart, and talented, and Michael Welch is clearly smitten with you." Lily squeezed her hand. "He'd be lucky to have you, and from the looks of it, he knows it."

Carly scoffed. "Yeah, right. Have you seen the women he dates? I'm easily twice their size."

"Stop it, that's enough. You like him, and he clearly likes you. Anyone with half a brain can see that. No more of this 'woe is me, I'm not good enough for the amazing Michael Welch' nonsense. If you don't at least try to tell him how you really feel, I'll never believe that you actually want to be happy."

Wow. Was Lily right? Had she sabotaged her chance at happiness? She'd told herself that the relationship was a charade, that none of it was real, but maybe she'd just been guarding her heart against disappointment. He'd never given her any reason to believe that she wasn't the kind of woman he'd be interested in. Too scared to take a chance, she'd let herself believe that the risk wasn't worth the possibility of heartbreak. Little did she realize that heartbreak could come either way, whether she guarded her heart or handed it to Michael on a silver platter.

"If he didn't have feelings for you, he wouldn't have thought twice about staying behind to shoot the pilot. He asked if you wanted him to stay because part of him probably wanted you to say yes."

"But I didn't say yes because I was too sure that he didn't care."

She watched the screen as they kissed in the microbrewery parking lot, like a couple in love, and she saw what she'd tried so hard to deny. It was real.

•••

Michael locked the door of his temporary L.A. apartment behind him and dropped his keys on the kitchen bar as he headed straight for the refrigerator. Takeout leftovers and a six-pack of Amber Wolf lager lined the metal shelves, and he pulled a bottle out. As he pulled the cap off and took the first ice-cold drink of the brew, he tried not to think of Carly and the brief time they'd spent together. Some days, if he concentrated on his new show hard enough, he could pretend it never happened, if only for a few hours. The nights were hard, though, when he returned to an empty apartment with nothing to keep him company but his memories.

Damn, he was losing it. How many different ways could he tell himself that she didn't care if he stayed or left? She couldn't have made it any clearer that her feelings for him hadn't changed one bit. He dropped onto the scratchy furnished sofa and flipped on the television as he toed off his shoes. If he had half a brain, he'd focus on making sure the new pilot was a success. The last thing he needed was to tank another show. Second chances were few and far between, especially for guys like him.

Freaking *Sugar Shock* came on, and he found himself unable to change the channel, even though he'd seen their episode already. Considering how often they reran programs, he was liable to see it twenty times before it cycled out of rotation. He smiled as he watched the blue icing splatter across his chef's whites, the look of disgust on Carly's face as she talked about him in her confessional interview, and the way he laughed off her irritation. They danced in the kitchen as Antonio watched, and a lump formed in his throat.

They were perfect together, a beautiful pair, and he'd let her slip through his fingers without really trying to keep her. Watching the two of them glide around the cramped space, her trusting him with the final dip, he could practically feel her in his arms again. Closing his eyes, he could see her, close enough to kiss the faint freckles sprinkled across her nose. He'd replayed their night of passion together a hundred times, could recall the feel of her silky auburn hair in his hands and the way her body fit against his perfectly. He'd never forget the need he saw in her eyes, either to help her through the show or to take her in the bed they'd shared.

Why was he watching this? It was impossible to deny his feelings for her when they played out on his television, night after night. His cell phone buzzed, rattling against the glass coffee table, and he muted the show to answer.

"What's up, hoss?" Rusty Grainger's robust twang came through the line.

"Rusty! How are you, man?" Michael settled back against the cushions.

"Good, good, can't complain, and nobody would listen if I did." He laughed at his own joke. "Listen, I wanted to see if you had some simpler cake ideas for the groom's cake that you could send over."

"Carly's having trouble with the cake?" That was a surprise. Their styles were wildly different, but he'd never met another baker as talented as she was. His instructions were clear, and the design was well within her ability.

"Naw, man, Carly's a trooper, but I don't want to lose her, too. This would strictly be for backup, just in case."

"What? Why would you lose her?" He sat up on the couch. Surely they weren't going to cancel their contract because he'd backed out?

"Sequoia is worried about the karma or the energy or something, dude. She thinks that Carly's tears over your breakup will fall into the cake batter and infuse it with sorrowful energy or something. Her words, not mine, obviously. She made Carly do some kind of cleansing ritual, but if anything goes wrong, I think Sequoia will see it as a sign and call the whole thing off. It won't take much." He chuckled.

"Are you serious?" And there were tears over the breakup?

"As a heart attack. I think it'll be fine, but I don't want to take any chances. Sequoia always worries about negative emotions affecting our union."

"Her words, I guess?" Michael wanted to laugh, but he couldn't believe that Sequoia's beliefs might affect Carly's job. Or that Carly had a broken heart. As much as it gutted him to think of her in pain, a part of him hoped that she really was brokenhearted over letting him go.

"You know it." He could hear the smile in Rusty's voice, his words infused with affection for his quirky fiancée. Michael understood, and it hurt like hell that he didn't have Carly around to love regardless of her quirks.

Sure, he told her he'd stay if she wanted, but now he realized that was a cop-out. If he'd been man enough to admit that he'd fallen for her, she might have stomped all over his heart, but at least he would've put it out there. Instead, he'd put the burden on her to decide the fate of their relationship, and probably pushed her into thinking that he didn't care what she did. He was a coward, and he'd lost a good woman because of it. Not only that, but he'd compromised her professional life, too.

Chapter Twelve

Carly swirled icing onto the last of three-dozen perfect but boring pink princess-themed cupcakes for a little girl's birthday party and boxed them neatly into Caketopia's signature lavender boxes. Once they were stacked neatly on her worktable, she threw away the plastic piping bag and washed the decorating tip, trying to tell herself that she found just as much joy in providing beautiful cupcakes for a kid's birthday party as she did creating the Grainger-Rivers wedding cake. As the warm water sluiced over her hands and into the stainless steel sink, she reasoned that even if Sequoia Rivers was a kook, she might be onto something. Carly couldn't think of anything lately except losing Michael and how stupidly sad she was over the whole thing. But in her heart of hearts, she knew she'd done the right thing. He was meant for more than working at a bakery, and no matter how much she wanted him for herself, she had to let him go.

She dried off the metal decorating tip and returned it to her case. Everything in its place. Layla came in, knocking on the doorframe as she walked, and seated herself at Carly's worktable.

"These for the Sophie Chambers party?" She indicated the stack of bakery boxes.

"Yep, just finished up with those and ready for the next order." Carly busied herself drying her hands and avoided eye contact with her employee.

"Great, because we're backed up. I'll take these to the refrigerated case for you, and then we have something like a dozen new orders to talk about." Layla looked at Carly over the tops of her red-framed glasses. "What really happened with Michael Welch in Los Angeles?"

Carly's shoulders slumped. "Nothing happened. You know as much as I do, really."

"I doubt that. You look too depressed for a woman who just got the job of a lifetime and doesn't have to share the spotlight." Layla's gaze was pointed, unflinching. "You want to tell me what's going on? I thought it was really strange when you told me that you were together, and even more strange when you came back without him, but things are clearly much more serious than I thought. We can talk about it, if you want."

Carly blew out a breath and shot a glance to the door. Seeing that it was closed, she pulled her second barstool out and sat by Layla at her worktable. "You can't tell anyone, okay?" When her employee nodded, she continued. "When we pitched the wedding, Sequoia wanted to hire us because she thought we were a couple. Before I could correct her, Michael jumped in and told her that we were, and after that, I just went with it."

Layla paused, obviously formulating a response, and tapped the worktable. "Okay, as absurd as that is, I can understand why you went along with it, and it makes much more sense than you falling for a guy you used to hate. I'm sure it seemed harmless enough at the time. Nobody could've predicted that you'd end up back on that game show or that Michael's showbiz career would get a second life."

"Thank you. I feel like a complete idiot for not just correcting her that day and letting the situation play out however it would have." She slumped on the barstool and stared at her hands.

"What I can't figure out," she put a hand over Carly's, "is why you're so depressed now. Are you feeling overwhelmed now that Michael's not working the wedding? Is this too much pressure for one job?"

Unbidden, tears welled in Carly's eyes and fell in fat puddles on the table. With a shuddering breath, she pulled herself together the best she could. "No, that's not all."

Her voice was a raspy whisper, and a hot flush crept into her cheeks. Layla was her friend, but their relationship had always been completely professional, the lines between employer and employee strictly respected.

Understanding lit her eyes. "So, it's safe to say that your little charade with Michael took a turn toward reality when you two were in L.A.? I can't say that I'm surprised, you know. I watched your episode of *Sugar Shock*. There's no faking the way you two look at one another." Layla stood, the barstool scraping against the tile as it moved. "Well, I wish I could tell you that I could handle everything so you could go home and sort this out, but you're just too darn successful. There are two more orders that have to be finished by the afternoon. If we each take one, you can take off a little early and sort this out. I'll cover for you after that. It could give you a little time to pull yourself together and come back in tomorrow ready to work. We'll sink without you here."

She patted Carly's shoulder and left without another word. Feeling like a fool for crying in front of an employee and letting her emotions affect her work, Carly wiped her eyes and straightened her spine. She was a professional, and it was time she acted like one. With a deep cleansing breath, she told herself to save the tears for home, then made her way to the front to pick up the order sheets.

• • •

Michael arrived at the studio, dragging himself in when he should be feeling on top of the world. The pilot schedule was ticking along at a faster pace than he ever would have thought, the production staff welcomed his input at every stage, and by all standards, the show was a dream job. If the pilot went well, there was no reason to think the network wouldn't pick them up. Everything was going his way, for once, but all he could think about was what he'd lost. He reported to hair and makeup, dropped into his chair, and sipped from the paper cup of coffee he picked up on the way. His stylist came in, toting an oversized bag full of products and equipment, on a cloud of coffee breath and cigarette smoke. Simply delightful. Nothing at all like the sweet vanilla-frosting scent of Carly.

"Good morning, love," she chirped. "Ready for your big day?"

"I'm ready to rock." He tried to summon an ounce of the enthusiasm he should feel, but nothing meant much lately. She got to work on his hair while she chattered about the other Cuisine Network personalities. He smiled and made the appropriate noises, relieved that he wasn't expected to contribute much to the conversation.

"Hey, you know, I do know you. I was wracking my brain, trying to figure it out. You were on *Sugar Shock*." She snapped her fingers and grinned.

"Guilty as charged," he said as he spread his hands out.

"So where's the pretty girlfriend of yours?" She didn't recognize him from the season he won. She'd seen him during the past week. Crap.

"Back in Dallas." Not sure how much to reveal to the hair-and-makeup lady, he kept it vague. Maybe she'd drop it.

No such luck. "What? How can you stand being here while she's all the way in Texas?"

"When opportunity knocks, I answer." He shrugged. "I got the chance to shoot the pilot, so I stayed here, and she went back home. The rest is history, I guess."

Somewhat deflated, she finished his stage makeup. "What a shame. I hope you two kids make it through the separation. That's a lot of distance to overcome, but if you're committed, you can do it. All done, love. Knock 'em dead out there."

He'd meant the quip about opportunity knocking as a light remark, but he sounded like an ass and he knew it. He'd ruined everything, not just for him, but for Carly as well. Today's segments would test his professionalism, because he sure as hell didn't feel like wowing the audience. The stylist packed up her supplies while he watched himself in the mirror, made up and camera-ready. And depressed as hell. With herculean effort, he pushed out of the chair and got to his feet, his internal pep talk on a continuous loop. He'd given up everything for this job. Might as well make it shine.

Michael took his place behind the counter in the sound stage kitchen, which could've been plucked from a big suburban home and dropped into the studio. Production staff and crew shuffled around the set, flipping switches, adjusting equipment, pointing and checking lights. So much of working on a show was hurry up and wait. He'd forgotten that decidedly unglamorous fact while he was busy wishing for this life. After his years at The Clubhouse, where he was always busy, standing around on set twiddling his thumbs was mind-numbing.

The director finally arrived, striding in at a brisk clip while his assistant trailed behind him, obviously trying to keep up. The show's director was a robust man, clearly accustomed to taking charge and having others follow without question. Michael straightened and held out his hand as they approached. The assistant pressed a button on her earpiece and spoke into it as she turned away from them.

"Good morning, Michael. It's so good to see you back with the network," the director said.

Michael pumped his hand and returned the greeting. "Great to be here, thanks. I'm looking forward to getting back to work." Was he, really?

"Wonderful. As we discussed, you'll talk the audience through your cake design today, using the pieces that we already baked and the ingredients you requested. You should find them assembled and ready to go on the shelves beneath the counter. The appeal of a show like this is the artistry and craft. I doubt most of our viewers intend to work along with you at home to make these cakes, but we're going to include the recipes on the website, so you'll need to give at least some instruction. Most of all, though, we want to see your personality. We have a dozen dessert shows on the network, so you've got to show the executives what makes yours worth picking up. Don't be afraid to take chances."

With a firm pat on the arm, the director was off to finalize the setup. Michael scanned the shelves beneath the counter. There was a prebaked cake waiting for him to pull out of the cold oven, but he was to assemble and mix the batter from the premeasured ingredients waiting for him. The hot stage lights burned above him, and he squinted, seeing only moving figures in the shadows beyond them. The call for quiet on the set went out, and after a count, theme music began. A surprising surge of excitement flew through him at the sound of the music, a piece clearly meant to reflect his rebel reputation with its heavy rock undertones. He'd focused on what he'd lost so much in the last week that he forgot what a rush shooting his own show could be. He didn't have to fake the wide smile that spread across his face when the music faded and the show started.

"Welcome to *Around the World in Thirteen Cakes* with Michael Welch. Of course, I'm your host, Michael Welch." He winked at the camera, finding his rhythm and remembering all the old tricks he used the first time around. "I'm going to take you on a vacation every week. We'll explore new places and reflect the flavors and cultures we find in a cake that we create together. How does that sound?"

He'd learned on the first pilot how to act like he was chatting with a friend in the kitchen, but it was still strange to hold a one-way conversation with the camera in a room full of people. It came easier this time, but it took a lot of energy to maintain interest without a co-host.

"For our first trip, we decided to stay close to home and take you around sunny, beautiful, Los Angeles, California." It wasn't his home, but it would be for the time being. "When you live here, it's easy to forget how many wonderful things there are to see. Did you watch the Valentine's Day episode of *Sugar Shock*? You might have seen a familiar face," he said with a grin. "If you missed it, be sure to catch it before it's gone, because it's a good one. I visited the show with my smokin' hot girlfriend where we were kindly invited to help judge the semifinalist round."

Could he still call her his girlfriend?

"Throughout the season, I'm going to amp it up and give you some of my secret recipes for my mouth-watering signature cakes, so be sure to keep watching. Today, we're going to go with a classic to get you started. I'm going to ease you into things with the most delicious vanilla cake you've ever tasted. Think vanilla is boring? Think again, because there is nothing boring about a classic when it's perfect. Throw away your boxed mixes and get out your pens and paper, because I'm going to take the mystery out of baking from scratch today. Let's get started."

He pulled out the bowls, premeasured ingredients, and equipment from beneath the counter and assembled everything in order. "Before you start any cake, make sure you have everything. You don't want to get halfway through before you discover that you don't have enough eggs, right? Speaking of eggs, take four of them and mix with two cups of granulated sugar." He walked the audience through the recipe, adding his own flourishes of personality along the way. "Just bake at three-fifty for about thirty minutes, and there you have it. See? Making a cake is easy as pie. The secret is to make it fresh and to use the best ingredients you can afford. Don't worry about adding anything, because this vanilla is traditional for a reason." Before he met Carly, Michael never cared much for classics, but he had definitely developed a taste for them since.

He poured the batter into prepared cake pans and slid them into the cold oven. They would run commercials and then show him pulling a finished cake out of the oven, ready to decorate. They'd use some generic film of L.A. attractions, but he knew they'd show a lot of footage from his stint on *Sugar Shock* with Carly. Not only would he be forced to watch it again, he'd have to make witty comments about what the audience saw. Using footage that had already been shot by another network property saved the show a tremendous amount of money. He'd trek to more exotic locales if the show was picked up.

They'd splice together the baking, decorating, and travel portions of the show after filming. He pulled the already baked, cooled, and ready-for-decorating cake from the oven and faced the camera. "Let your cakes cool before you attempt to decorate. The last thing you want is to pour time into baking the perfect cake only to have the frosting melt all over it." He leveled the cakes and positioned one on a turntable before slathering the top with a generous layer of buttercream frosting. After setting the second cake on top, careful to line them up, he quickly applied the second layer of frosting, leaving a clean canvas for his masterpiece.

"Carly and I were lucky enough to celebrate Valentine's Day early this year, back on the set of the show where we met. When most people think of L.A., they think of movie stars, sunshine, and television. When I think of this beautiful city, though, love is all that comes to mind. It's where I met Carly, and while we fell in love hundreds of miles away in Dallas, we've had some wonderful times here."

He carefully blended red gel coloring into a bowl of white icing until it was a gorgeous shade of pink. "I'll share a little trick of the trade with you. When you fill a piping bag to decorate a cake, use a glass to hold it. That way you're much less likely to end up with a sticky mess all over your countertops." He opened a disposable piping bag into a glass and spooned the icing inside. As he piped perfect hearts over the smooth white surface of his cake, he wondered what Carly was working on.

Probably something a lot like this, something beautiful and important to the person who'd ordered it, something she'd put her unmistakable mark of quality on. Was she thinking of him? Did she miss him and wish they were working on the wedding together?

"And, boom, there you have it. A special cake for an unforgettable Valentine's Day. Find *Around the World in Thirteen Cakes* online at the Cuisine Network for recipes, special offers from our sponsors, and video from today's show. Thank you for watching, and be sure to follow us on Twitter. Here's hoping that you bake your cake and eat it, too."

The scene ended, and the staff photographer swooped in to light the shot of the cake. They'd post it on the show's website along with a recipe, but the cake would probably be thrown away as soon as they were finished with it. It had been handled by too many people since coming out of the oven and making its television debut. Like so many other things in his life, it looked great, but it was all for show.

Chapter Thirteen

Carly hummed to herself as she squeezed a perfectly uniform scalloped edge along the sharp lines of a cake she was making for a couple's tenth anniversary party. Led Zeppelin's *IV* filled the workroom, and she nodded her head along with the hard-driving rhythm of "Black Dog." No more Pachelbel for a while, not until she could make it through one day without turning into a weepy mess at the thought of weddings and romance.

Sequoia Rivers ducked her head through the doorway, softly offering a greeting and pulling Carly's attention away from the cake.

"Carly? I knocked, but I guess you didn't hear me." She grinned as she nodded toward the small stereo. "Now I see why. I love Led Zeppelin."

"Hey, Sequoia. What's up?" With any luck, she'd soon be able to see Sequoia without thinking of Michael.

"I came in so Layla could show me the cupcake bar setup, and I wanted to stop by and check on you. Were you able to do the sage smudge cleansing in your apartment?"

Carly and Lily had done the cleansing, from one end of her apartment to the other, concentrating on the corners where negative energy tended to accumulate. They'd giggled through the cleansing, using the ritual more as an excuse to get together than anything else, but part of Carly wanted to believe it would work. If there was anything that could lighten the negativity holding her down, some way to open her up to possibility, then she would try it.

"I did. Thank you for thinking of me."

"Girl, I think of you all the time. It breaks my heart that you lost your love in the midst of my elation, and I want you to be happy." Sequoia settled on the stool next to her and cupped Carly's hand between hers. Sequoia's eyes were wide, sincerity shining through. This was too much, really. Carly had created this lie, and it was her responsibility to live with the fallout once it disintegrated. Sequoia's unswerving sympathy was both unearned and undeserved.

"I'll be fine, Sequoia. Please don't worry yourself with me when all you should be thinking about is your wedding." Carly pulled her hand away and sat up straighter. Pasting a bright smile on her face, she tried to look like a woman who was well on her way to recovering from heartbreak.

"Do you think the cleansing helped?"

Sequoia looked so hopeful that Carly found herself nodding. "Definitely. I didn't realize how bad I felt until it lifted."

"That negative energy can be so oppressive." Sequoia nodded sagely. "I hope it helped to clear the path to happiness." She pulled her oversized tote bag off her shoulder and rummaged around inside. Carly briefly wondered if Sequoia could actually fit in it and smiled to herself.

Sequoia pulled out an elaborately decorated deck of cards and pushed her bag across the table to make space. "Would you mind? I'd love to read your cards."

First the sage smudge, now tarot card readings. What was next? A juice cleanse and a vow of silence? As much as she'd like to dismiss Sequoia's beliefs as quackery, she was curious and found herself agreeing despite her misgivings.

Sequoia smiled beatifically and spread the cards in a neat row. "Awesome. Let's do a simple reading, then. Pick six cards."

Carly plucked six cards from the line, and with each, Sequoia told her what they represented. "How you feel about yourself now, what you want most at this moment, your fears, what you have going for you, what's working against you, and outcome."

She flipped the cards over to reveal the faces, and smiled, her eyes glittering with possibility. "This is good, Carly, really good."

It didn't look good, more like warriors, a devil, and a dead guy, but Carly waited for the explanation. Sequoia set them out in the order that she chose them.

"The chariot. It means that you feel like everything is a battle right now, but don't worry because good news is on its way." She pointed to a creepy card and Carly cringed, sure it was bad news. "This one is judgment. What you want now more than anything is to close this chapter in your life and move on." Well, that was pretty accurate. Moving on from the agony of losing Michael before she realized she wanted him would be heavenly. "The next card is for your fears, and we have the devil. You're afraid that a passionate desire is out of control. You think it's addictive and bad for you, which may or may not be true." And that would be her wild attraction to Michael, she supposed.

"Now we have what you've got going for you, and it's a good one, justice. You can expect a karmic reward for good deeds you've done in the past, even when it seems like you don't deserve favor. As for what's working against you," Sequoia said as she pointed to the fifth card, "we have the world. Don't worry, that doesn't mean that the world is against you. It means that fear holds us back from opportunities. Only you can decide if you let it." A truer statement had never been made. "And finally, the outcome card." Sequoia pointed to the sixth and final card, and Carly cringed. It was a guy hanging by his feet, clearly dead or at least seriously injured. "This is the hanged man. You can stop holding your breath, because it doesn't mean that you'll end up like this guy. It represents a time of passage in your life, when you have to decide what or who must be given up. It points to self-sacrifice being necessary for your happiness, and that's never easy."

Amazed at how insightful a deck of cards could be, Carly watched as Sequoia tucked them back into their box. "Thank you. That was weird, but also kind of soothing."

"I hope it'll help you in your search for answers. I think the important thing about tarot is how you personally interpret your reading. It's an art, not a science, and every card can mean different things for different people." Sequoia pulled Carly into a hug. The actress pulled back, leaving the space between them scented with patchouli, and held her by the shoulders. "I'm telling you this with peace and love. I don't know what happened between you and Michael, but you're meant to be together. I hope you find your way back to one another."

Determined not to cry over her fake relationship in front of the woman unknowingly responsible for bringing them together, Carly slipped from her grasp. "We'll see. Whatever's meant to be, will be."

"Sure, but we also have a hand in our own destinies, don't you think?" Sequoia pulled her bag over her shoulder and stood. "Sometimes we have to go after what we want, rather than waiting for the universe to provide it."

Of course Carly didn't expect the universe to drop Michael back in her lap, but what could she do? "You're right. Thank you for the reading, and for everything."

"Any time. Let me know if there's anything else I can do."

Outside of giving her the courage to tell Michael how she felt, there was little Sequoia could do for Carly. What she'd dismissed as kookiness at first had shown itself to be the way Sequoia lived her life and defined her personal code. After spending time with her, Carly could see that Sequoia was a genuinely caring person much more enlightened than she was.

"Thanks, Sequoia. And I want you to know that your wedding is our top priority. I'm not going to think about Michael or our problems when I'm working on your cakes." To her surprise, she was sincere. Sequoia's beliefs were close to her heart, and Carly respected them.

"Don't worry about me. You need to spend some serious time thinking about what you want and how to get it. Make that your wedding gift to me, okay?"

She swallowed against the lump in her throat. The kindness and positive energy must be getting to her. "Okay," she managed.

What she wanted was for Michael to come back, to confess his unexpected but complete love and devotion to her, and for them to bake the Grainger-Rivers wedding cakes side by side. Her mother always shook her head at such silly fantasies, saying, "If wishes were horses, then beggars would ride." Instead, she'd suggest ways in which Carly might make her dreams come true, rather than sitting around hoping for things to work out. Perhaps it was time to saddle up, lasso her troubles, and wrestle them to the ground.

• • •

"So, why can't you call him?" Lily sipped a diet cola and watched Carly pack from her perch on the vanity stool in Carly's bedroom.

"I don't have his phone number, and the only person I know who has it is freaking Rusty Grainger, who would probably wonder why I didn't have my boyfriend's cell number." Carly searched her closet for the jeans she wanted to pack. Sequoia was right; she couldn't wait for the universe to hand her happiness. This was crazy, but living the rest of her life knowing that she'd let love slip from her grasp without even trying to go for it was worse.

"What are you going to do when you get there?" Lily sat up as though she were settling in for a juicy soap opera.

Carly blew the hair off her forehead and pulled the jeans off the hanger. "Honestly? I have no idea. I hope that we'll see each other and then it will come to me. If it seems like he's on a completely different page, then I'll figure something out, make something up about the groom's cake or something."

"You already know what I think. Two people don't look at each other like you do unless there's something between them. Surely you didn't imagine everything."

"I don't think so, but he's a lot more comfortable with stuff like that than me. I might show up and get laughed out of the place. Wait, scratch that. If I get any hint that he's not that into me, I'm going to bail on the plan. Sorry if that seems like a waste of your miles, but I can't stand the thought of sticking around to face rejection."

Lily dismissed her with a wave of her hand. "If you had any idea how many airline miles I have, you wouldn't worry about it for another second. I'm just glad to help, and I hope I'm part of your big love story when it's all said and done. Be sure to tell your future children how I made it possible for you two to get together."

Carly packed a couple of extra t-shirts and zipped up her overnight bag. "Don't get ahead of yourself. But seriously, thank you, Lil. I am scared to death, but I couldn't do this without you."

Zipping off on a moment's notice with no plan was completely out of character, but so was falling for Michael Welch. What could she do, ask him to come back home with her? She couldn't ask him to drop out of his own show to come back and work at a bakery. The only real way they could be together would be if she found work in Los Angeles and moved there to be with him. Maybe it was time to branch out and open another bakery or start teaching classes. She'd be leaving a lot behind, but her skills allowed her to work anywhere that people ate cake. Things were getting deep, but she'd figure everything out as she went.

• • •

Carly had no idea how to find Michael's apartment or wherever he was living when she reached L.A., but she knew where he worked.

Cursing herself for not sucking it up and asking someone from his shop for his number, she pushed through the heavy revolving door at Cuisine Network. When she'd gratefully accepted Lily's offer of airline miles and taken off without a second thought, it seemed like a romantic idea, like something they could tell their grandchildren about one day. Now, here in the cold reality of what she'd done, showing up unannounced just felt stupid. What if he wasn't working today? Worse, what if he didn't want to see her? The lobby buzzed with activity, as uniformed crewmen and suit-clad executives crossed the marble floor at breakneck speeds. She seemed to be the only person here who didn't know exactly where to go. The reception desk sat at the end of the lobby, a beacon of calm in the sea of scrambling people.

Knowing she couldn't turn back without at least trying to find him, she approached the reception desk. An older man with kind, watery blue eyes looked up from his bank of screens and raised his eyebrows in greeting.

"Good afternoon, I'm looking for someone who works on a show here. Well, it's not actually a show yet; it's a pilot. And I don't know what it's called." *Crap. Now what?* "And I don't know if they're shooting here or out on location, or done already," she rambled until the man put his hand up to stop her.

"Do you know this mystery man's name, at least, young lady?" he teased her, his voice was tinged with amusement.

"Yes. Michael Welch." Glad she had one piece of information, she stood up a little straighter, glancing around the beautifully decorated lobby as the man scanned the information on his computer screen.

"You're in luck, my dear. Mr. Welch is indeed here today, and they are shooting in Studio Seven." He pointed across the lobby toward a walkway. "It's a closed set, but perhaps you can speak with the receptionist over there and leave a message."

"Great, thank you so much." She was jittery, practically vibrating with excitement and nerves.

After he entered her in the visitor's log, she followed his directions, heart racing, toward the studio. As she darted between the people crowding the lobby, she mentally rehearsed what she'd say when she found Michael. Now that the moment was close, reality hovered over her, threatening to crash. He had managed to go from being a thorn in her side to the man she couldn't stop thinking of. Telling him that she'd fallen for him would require major guts—something she didn't count among her strengths. With any luck, emotion would carry her through the moment, and she'd be able to share her feelings without humiliating herself. How he would react was a whole other mystery, one she hadn't given much thought to when she was throwing her overnight bag together and heading out of town on the first flight she could book. No time to worry now. Studio Seven was right in front of her.

Chapter Fourteen

"I've got good news and bad news, Michael." Craig Greenfield, an *Around the World* staffer, leaned against the studio set counter and sipped from a cup of steaming coffee.

"Give it to me." Michael drank his own coffee, wincing as his too-big gulp scorched his throat. He dropped onto one of the prop barstools and tried to project an air of confidence. Bad news at this stage couldn't be anything he wanted to hear, but knowing that appearance was everything, he hid his apprehension.

"We looked over the footage you shot the other day, and the good news is that the camera loves you. We're still confident that we made the right choice in picking you for this show. You've got that special something that we look for in our hosts."

"That sounds great so far." Afraid he sounded too hearty, too bright, he sipped his coffee and let the executive continue.

"So, here's the bad news." Craig blew out a long breath. "The show is boring as hell. I'm sorry to have to say that, but there's no way around it." He held up his hands in surrender.

Boredom was the kiss of death. If Michael were honest, he'd say the same thing. Even as he was filming, he knew the content was tepid regardless of how charming he managed to be.

"People aren't going to tune in to watch you bake and decorate a cake. They can get recipes anywhere, and not even your good looks are enough to get people to give up their reality show fixes." The executive laughed at his little joke. "But it's not all bad news. We believe in this project, so we've brainstormed some ways to fix it."

Okay, so it wasn't all over. At least they were willing to put a little more time into it before trashing the pilot and sending him on his way. "Cool, what do you have in mind?"

"First, and probably most important, we think you need a co-host. The most appealing parts of your *Sugar Shock* footage are the scenes with you and Carly Piper. We've got someone we like for the spot coming in today, and we hope that will help a lot. You've just got to pray that there's an ounce of the same chemistry between you and the new girl as there was between you and Ms. Piper."

A co-host was probably a good idea. He'd heard it before, and he'd learned his lesson last time after stubbornly insisting that he be the sole star of his own show. Once the sting of shooting his doomed pilot had worn off, he'd recognized that he'd work better as half of a duo. But he and Carly were magic together, and no random girl they brought in to work with him would match with him as perfectly. Maybe they could fake it, make it look good for the cameras. It wouldn't be like the *Sugar Shock* episodes, but he hoped it would come off as good enough.

"That sounds fine. Anything else?"

"Assuming that the co-host works out, we think a lot of the excitement necessary to carry the show will come out when we pump up the content to jive more with the original concept. We cut corners to save money on the pilot, but we can't sell the show with *Sugar Shock* footage and a generic Valentine's Day cake like we'd hoped. We'd love to showcase your favorite recipes on the show's website, but the episode cakes have to be more like your trademark Michael Welch designs and less like a cake-baking clinic."

In a nutshell, the only thing that was right about the show was that he was handsome enough to be on television. His cake was generic, the footage was boring, and the recipe was too commonplace to sell advertising. If they were going to turn it around, the co-host had to be one hell of a looker. Confidence was everything, so he went with it.

"Sounds great. When can I meet her?"

"She's in hair and makeup now, so it should be any minute. Whenever she's done, we'll get some test shots. She seems like a natural, and I think you're really going to like her."

That was fast. He couldn't expect to audition actresses alongside the producers, but if the whole idea was to find someone he'd have amazing Carly-level chemistry with, he'd think they'd want a little input from him. It was just another reminder that he wasn't in charge. His name was on the show, but only because they put it there. Time to play ball.

A stunning blonde approached, high heels clicking on the studio floor's smooth surface with each confident step of her mile-long legs. A scarlet dress hugged every inch of her body, highlighting the undeniable fact that she was virtually flawless. As she got closer, the perfection in her features didn't fade, but became more pronounced. She threw a dazzling smile at the executive and stretched a perfectly manicured hand toward Michael.

They shook hands, and he was struck by how soft her skin was. Her practiced smile revealed perfectly straight, television-white teeth, probably veneers. "You must be Michael Welch. I'm a huge fan. I remember you from your season of *Sugar Shock* and seriously love your cake designs. I'm Kaitlin Myers, and it's so nice to meet you."

"You too, Kaitlin. Nice to have you on board." Her eyes were an unusual turquoise, fringed by lashes too long and lush to be natural. She must be wearing colored contacts.

"Kaitlin's background is in modeling, and she's getting started in television. She's clearly not a chef, but she's definitely talented. It'll be interesting to see how you two interact on set." The executive swept a meaningful look at her miniscule waistline. "We're thinking that she'll really shine on the show's travel segments more than anything, and maybe it'll help to have someone to talk to besides the camera when you're filming the decorating portions."

"Hey, I'm willing to do whatever it takes." Michael injected his voice with enthusiasm, but he worried that adding Kaitlin to the show just for eye candy wasn't going to enhance the content. Women formed the majority of this kind of show's audience, and he couldn't imagine many wanted to watch some random blonde stand around while he made cakes she wouldn't eat. With any luck, she'd at least be interesting or charming.

"Great, so let's get some test promo shots today. It's a little backwards, I know, since we don't have any film footage with the two of you, but we're hammering out details to get you out on location. We're going to redo pretty much everything, but we'll use the cake-baking and decorating footage for the website, so it's not a waste."

He led Michael and Kaitlin to a photo shoot set in the studio, where they posed against a generic background, the network logo, and a mock-up of *Around the World in Thirteen Cakes*'s logo. Kaitlin was clearly skilled in her profession, requiring minimal direction. She laughed, smiled adoringly, and playfully wrung Michael's neck for the camera. Every shot was designed to make them look like old friends and perfect partners. He went along with it, but felt nothing for the gorgeous blonde putting her hands all over him. When they finished and headed toward the studio set kitchen to shoot sample tape, it was a relief to be back in his wheelhouse.

Behind the counter, Michael loosened up and turned on the charm. He ran through the generic cooking-show dialogue they'd prepared, tossing questions and comments at Kaitlin as she tittered and stood by looking like she'd never been in a kitchen before. She flashed a mega-watt smile at the camera when appropriate, and looked what she probably thought was adorably confused as he talked about baking.

It was clear why the network chose her. Kaitlin would be goofy and self-deprecating enough so that the women who watched their show would like her. Any men who stumbled onto the channel would be easy enough to snare. Her legs went on for miles, her face was the kind most guys would like to wake up next to, and she had doe-eyed adoration down to a science. It could be a slam dunk but for one small problem. There was nothing happening between them. Not even the hint of a spark. Nothing. He touched her arm and delivered precooked dialogue, knowing that he'd feel nothing but trying for that familiar coziness the network was looking for.

They wanted Carly-and-Michael chemistry, that special something that happens once in a lifetime. They weren't going to find it between Michael and Kaitlin, but maybe it would translate differently on television. His heart wasn't in it, though, and the longer he stood on set with her laughing at his jokes and batting her eyelashes, the more he wished she were Carly.

He didn't want a tall blonde with perfect hair and teeth. He wanted peachy skin, wild gorgeous hair, and wicked sense of humor. Kaitlin likely made him look good on camera, but Carly made him a better man. He wanted the perfect fit and the crackling chemistry, not the manufactured beauty and impeccable timing of some model-slash-actress.

• • •

Carly took a deep, steadying breath outside Studio Seven. The receptionist had recognized her name from *Sugar Shock* and gave her a pass to visit the set, so the only thing stopping her was nerves. Heart-pounding, sweat-inducing nerves. She ran her fingers through her hair, wishing that she'd found a ladies' room and freshened up before bolting down to the studio. Not that fresh makeup and perfect hair would win his heart if he wasn't interested. He'd seen her made up for television, first thing waking up in the morning, and everything in between. And after that one crazy night, he'd pretty much seen everything there was to see.

She peeked through the tiny window on the door leading into the studio, ready to push the handle and walk in, ready to get out of her own way for once and take charge of her happiness. What she saw stopped her internal pep talk in its tracks. A beautiful blonde woman was draped over Michael, smiling at a man in a suit as she laughed at his jokes. She clearly adored him, and Carly knew she'd waited too long. He didn't belong to her anymore. He belonged with a beautiful, perfect woman like the one playfully slapping his shoulder on the other side of the door. Her trip to L.A. was nothing more than a fantasy that had gotten out of hand. She ripped the paper "visitor" sticker off her shirt and tossed it in the garbage as she rushed down the hall and far away from Studio Seven.

• • •

Kaitlin sashayed out of the studio, leaving Michael alone with Craig, who watched until she was out of sight. "Pretty great, huh?" The executive sat at the bar, like they were old friends talking in Michael's kitchen.

"She's beautiful, and she's clearly up for the job. She should be great on camera if today was any indication. I didn't feel a spark, though. That's what you were hoping for, right? That certain zing?"

"Out of the candidates we looked at, she's our best bet. I didn't see anyone else who came close, and I don't think we have time to run through the other ladies to see if you click with any of them."

"But if there's no chemistry, there's no chemistry, right?"

"Michael, I'll be straight with you. The show isn't going to fly with you on your own. That's a foregone conclusion, and we need to accept that. We didn't see it at first, but your appeal this time around comes from how charming you were with Carly. If we don't recreate that with another woman, I don't see the show getting picked up."

"Wouldn't the best candidate at least know something about cake? It didn't seem like Kaitlin had ever seen the inside of a kitchen before."

To his relief, the other man laughed. "You got me there. I'd love to have someone like Carly for your co-host, but to be honest, most actresses and models aren't also accomplished cake designers, and vice versa."

"So the best person for the job is Carly Piper, but we don't have her." He raked a hand across his face and mimed a thoughtful expression. "What if I could get her?"

The executive leaned back, a disbelieving smile spreading across his face. "Well, then that would clearly solve all our problems."

"All right. Don't make any moves until you hear from me then. I'll see what I can do."

"I'd be happy to call and make her an offer, get her to come out and test."

"Carly's special. She deserves a personal touch. I'm going to go get her."

• • •

Michael drummed his fingertips against the scratchy tweed of the couch in his temporary apartment as he waited for Rusty Grainger to answer the phone. "Hey, Rusty, it's Michael."

"Hey man, what's happening?" Rusty's hearty greeting reassured him that his disappearance from the wedding hadn't hampered their budding friendship.

"I have a huge favor to ask, so you'll have to trust me, but I think you're going to like what happens if my plan works out." He took a swig from a cold bottle of Amber Wolf lager and continued. "If I could promise you that something great will happen, even though it hasn't yet, could you convince Sequoia to take Carly off the groom's cake?"

"I don't know, man, she's pretty set on keeping her intentions pure, you know, staying honest. She's helped Carly a lot to get through the breakup, so she knows how sad she is. I doubt she'd be very eager to do anything that could hurt her more."

Carly needed help to get through the breakup? More reason to think that his plan would work. "I'm going to win Carly back, whatever it takes, so you can tell her that. I want to do the cake myself and surprise her when I show up in town."

"That might work. If you're sure that showing up would be a welcome surprise, I guess Sequoia might be okay with it. I know she'd be glad to see you two back together."

"I'm telling you, man, I'll do everything in my power to make sure it's a welcome surprise. So, just assure her that Carly will be okay once she sees the reason for being taken off the groom's cake. Have Sequoia give her a healing crystal or something. I'll be in town before you know it, and everything will be in motion."

"How can you be so sure she'll take you back, man? I haven't spent as much time with her as Sequoia has, but even I can tell that she is one sad little lady. You really did a number on her heart."

"Because when it's right, it's right, and I'm not ready to admit defeat. If she turns me down, it won't be because I'm not completely devoted to her. I'm willing to do whatever it takes to make her happy."

"I'll see what I can do, bro, but Sequoia's usually pretty set in her beliefs. I'll try my best, but I'd suggest you get your ass back to Dallas as quick as you can. Make it happen." He could hear the smile in Rusty's voice.

"Will do. See you soon." Michael ended the call and looked around the shabby prefurnished apartment, glad to be leaving it behind for a while. With any luck, he'd be coming back with Carly.

•••

Carly bobbed her head along to Led Zeppelin's "Misty Mountain Hop," heart lighter but not enough to return to her beloved Pachelbel's Canon, as she fitted her piping bag with the fat #789 decorating tip. Robert Plant sang about packing his bags for the Misty Mountains as she scooped white icing into the bag, and for the moment, she was content. Sequoia had swept through the halls of Caketopia and dismissed Carly from the groom's cake without explanation. The radiant bride refused to elaborate, but insisted that she still wanted Carly for the main cake. To her surprise, Carly was okay with it.

Until the wedding was over, Carly was determined to keep her thoughts positive and light. She might not hold the same spiritual beliefs as Sequoia, but she'd respect them and wouldn't allow her negative emotions or heartbreak over Michael to infect the wedding cake. It was actually a relief to be able to focus on the main cake. Without concentrating on Michael's designs, it was easier to pretend that her heart had never been broken.

With a steady hand, she squeezed a thick layer of white icing on the cakes, creating soft spirals of ribbons around the tops and then lining the sides. With her angled spatula, she smoothed the ribbons of icing into flawless planes, completely level without a crumb in sight. Few things gave her more pleasure than the stark white canvas of a perfectly smooth iced cake, ready for transformation. The possibilities stretched before her, compelling her to create something the bride would never forget. Being responsible for such an important, symbolic part of the wedding day was always an honor for Carly, but even more so now that she knew how much Sequoia valued every aspect of the ritual.

She'd complete the top layer of the fantasy fairy-tale cake first, the special cake they'd reserve to freeze and share on their first anniversary. It would be covered in delicate, lustrous bubbles and flowers. Carly pulled the premade spun sugar bubbles from their wax-paper-lined container and pressed them carefully into place, choosing only the most perfect spheres. She dusted gum paste calla lilies with edible pearl dust before arranging them within the bubbles to create a bouquet of shimmering flowers bursting from the center. After dotting perfect spheres of pearly fondant along the sides of the cake, the top layer was done. It was perfect, and Carly loved that her creation would be part of their story.

She hummed with satisfaction as she created a posh diamond-quilted pattern onto the other cakes and dotted each intersection with a tiny perfectly spun sugar sphere. Creations like this, where everything had to be perfect, made it easy to forget that there was a life outside her workroom, that anything could rival the attention required for the intense work. In keeping with her promise to project only love and light, if Michael crept into her mind, Carly shifted her thoughts to their happy times. She'd push aside the memory of him with the perfect blonde, the way he left her to pursue his career. She'd remember instead the way his lips felt on hers, how safe she felt in his arms, how quickly he'd captured her heart, how perfectly they fit together ...

Okay, no, she couldn't think of Michael. She'd instead focus on the cakes, perfect technique, and how it had been a long time since Robert Plant rock and rolled.

With a paintbrush stuck between her teeth, she pushed the cake layer on its turntable in a slow circle, checking for any imperfections and touching up the shimmery pearl powder where her sugar spheres needed extra sparkle. The cake would be magnificent, easily the most elaborate and beautiful she'd ever made. A gorgeous reflection of the union between two wonderful people who'd managed to find each other and not let go. Who worked together to sustain their relationship instead of letting fear and pride get in their way ...

Nope, none of that. She'd promised to keep her energy positive, and she meant to do just that. With a roll of her shoulders and a quick stretch, she took a cleansing breath and centered herself. She had hours to go before the cake would be finished, and none of them would be well spent brooding over Michael.

Chapter Fifteen

The raucous sound of The Rusty Grainger Band's new album filled the ballroom as dozens of vendors rushed throughout the space, finalizing details and running around like chickens with their heads cut off. Carly arranged the iridescent tulle snaking around the cake table to better support the delicate glass bubbles that dotted the surface, but she felt nothing but calm. She'd made the most complicated and breathtaking cake of her career, and she was pretty sure she'd managed to keep her tears out of the batter and her heartbreak out of the icing. It was a gorgeous confection, if she said so herself.

Anita, Carly's assistant for the event, showed up behind her, out of breath from running around checking on last-minute details. "Okay, so it turns out the photographer wants to shoot the cake as soon as he catches the couple coming into the reception. They want to get the whole tablescape, so we'll stage plates and forks as soon as he's done," Layla was across the ballroom fretting over the cupcake bar, working to avert any last-minute disasters.

"No problem." Carly checked her watch. "It looks like we have maybe ten minutes. I want to go touch up my hair and makeup, so please stay right here and don't let anything happen to the cake."

She rushed off across the venue's polished parquet floors, careful not to run into waitstaff or trip over wires and cables. The cake would be photographed for the couple's personal wedding album, but they would also sell the pictures to major celebrity news outlets, and there was a chance Carly would be featured alongside it. The hotel bathroom was empty, and Carly took the time to freshen up before the place was packed. The wedding should have ended already, and within minutes the reception ballroom would be full of guests waiting for the bride and groom to make their big entrance. She brushed her hair, trying hard not to remember the way Michael ran his fingers through it in the darkness of their hotel room. After pulling it into a tight bun and checking for escaped locks, she touched up her makeup so she'd look fresh for photographs. A quick turn in the mirror assured her that she was clean, pressed, and ready for primetime.

As she returned to her station, she briefly wondered why the groom's cake was nowhere near the wedding cake. She'd been too wrapped up in perfecting the wedding cake to look for it, but she did hope that whoever was in charge had produced something the newly minted Mr. and Mrs. Grainger would enjoy. The couple had been vague about their plans, simply assuring her that she needn't worry.

The DJ suddenly cut off Rusty's album midsong, and the lighting changed. The bright overheads were turned off and the ballroom was plunged into twilight as they switched to the event lighting. A disco ball turned the dance floor into a sea of swirling stars, an effect that usually reminded Carly of cheesy high school dances, but which felt magical tonight. She'd been to countless wedding receptions, some beautiful, some tacky, but none that could compare to the luxurious fantasy confection that awaited this bride and groom. Guests filed in, murmuring in appreciation and enjoying cocktails from cut crystal stemware as they waited for Rusty and Sequoia to arrive. Several guests drifted by the wedding cake and stopped to express their awe and give their compliments to the creator. Carly beamed, equal parts proud and elated to be noticed, with only the tiniest twinge of disappointment that she was alone.

The DJ announced the couple's imminent arrival, the lighting changed yet again, and Carly cracked up as Hank Williams Jr.'s "All My Rowdy Friends Are Coming Over Tonight" blasted through the speakers. Leave it to Rusty Grainger to take a posh, sophisticated event and put his own unique spin on it. Given

Sequoia's love for classic rock and her insistence that the event remind people of a fairy tale, Carly knew she had made a concession to the man she loved by walking into her wedding reception to old-school country music. As the DJ introduced them for the first time as man and wife, Rusty and Sequoia bounded in, smiling from ear to ear, hands linked and held high, to thundering cheers and applause.

A Clubhouse staffer wheeled the groom's cake over to the wedding-cake table, careful to avoid the reveling crowd. Had they found someone from Michael's shop to create his design? Carly shot the young assistant a sympathetic look as she wound through the guests, her teeth clenched and eyes narrowed, clearly doing her best to make sure nothing happened to the cake.

Carly did a double take when she finally glanced at the cake. The hair on the back of her neck stood up as she took in the unique design and incredible detail, all hallmarks of a Michael Welch original. Surely there was no way that anybody on his staff, no matter how talented, could make something like that. How long would it be before she stopped seeing him in everything? How many wedding receptions would it take before she could see an inventive cake and not feel like she'd had the wind knocked out of her? She wanted to do something, to spring into action and help the harried assistant stage her table, but the crowd was living up to their rowdy reputation and Carly dared not step away from her table. All eyes were on the couple, and it would be easy for someone to bump into her.

Still, the groom's cake was amazing. The baker had managed to capture the likeness of Rusty's dearest canine buddy, the aptly named Hank. His spunky little bull terrier was a well-known and often-photographed companion, as comfortable touring the country on a bus as he was at home in his own backyard. The shaped cake was more than just the dog, though, as the baker had incorporated Rusty's love of rockabilly culture and his flair for wild style in the colors and design splattered over the dog's coat. It was an amazing cake, from the realistic pillow the dog sat upon to the collar that was so detailed it looked like real nylon. It reminded Carly so much of Michael that it made her throat tighten to look at it. There would be no tears tonight, unless they were happy tears for the sweet bride who'd done so much for her.

Her assistant reported back, assuring her that everything was ready for the cake cutting later in the evening, including reserve sheet cakes in case the beautiful confection on the table didn't feed the entire guest list. The crowd parted, and Rusty and Sequoia's first dance as a married couple began. Few things touched Carly as much as the first dance. No matter how many receptions she attended, she was always moved by the sheer emotion inevitably shining through the couple's expressions. Rusty gazed down into Sequoia's eyes, completely focused on her, adoration written all over his face. For those three minutes, the couple would be in their own bubble, their new commitment shielding them from the disappointments and disasters that waited for them in the outside world. For the moment, nothing could touch them, and nothing else mattered.

As the song ended, the couple kissed and parted, to the cheers of the guests who then streamed onto the dance floor to join them. Rusty caught Carly's eye and winked. Surely there was someone else around her. Why on earth else would he be winking in her direction? She whipped around and was caught in a web of bergamot and leather, green eyes glittering in the low light. Michael. He encircled her wrist with his fingers and pulled her close, until his lips touched her ear.

"Can we talk?" His breath caressed her neck, and the stubble brushing against her skin sent goose bumps up her arms. "Anita, you're in charge of the cake," he instructed her assistant.

Somehow Carly managed to nod her head, as actual words refused to form in her brain, much less come out her lips. Her legs miraculously propelled her out of the ballroom and into the lobby, where she followed Michael across the gleaming marble floors to a dim corner. Hidden behind a giant floral arrangement, Michael pushed her against the wall, gently but insistently, until he was pressed against her.

"I'm going to kiss you, because it's all I've thought of for days, and then we'll talk. Sound good?" He whispered against her lips, close enough to touch but not close enough to satisfy the need that burst inside her. It felt so good to let go and follow his lead.

She managed a tiny nod before his lips claimed hers, fierce and primal in their urgency. He coaxed her lips open to deepen the kiss, and his familiar cinnamon taste flooded her memory so that her body responded without thought. Every moment they'd spent together came crashing her memory with an intensity she'd never imagined. He pulled her into his arms, and she answered with unashamed need, with a hungry enthusiasm she'd never shown any man. In his arms, she was home, and there was no need to hide.

As the kiss ended, her eyes stubbornly refused to open. Too afraid she'd find herself in a fantasy, she buried her face in the nook where his neck and shoulder met, the spot where she fit perfectly. He held her tight, assuring her that not only did he feel the exact same desperate longing, but that he was most definitely real and this was actually happening. Tilting her head up, she caught the bottom of his strong jaw with her lips and felt his body harden in response. With a shuddering breath, he stepped back, leaving inches between them that felt like miles.

"We still have to work this event. Can't get too carried away." His crooked grin told her that he wanted to take her away from the elegant lobby and find somewhere more private.

The haze of desire lifted, slowly, as they put more space between them, and her senses returned. "We?"

"You saw Rusty's cake, right? Did you think someone else made that?" He poked fun at his huge ego, sending the remaining tension in her shoulders into the ether.

"What are you doing here?"

"I came for you."

"You did?"

"I knew I was taking a chance, just showing up and surprising you, but I couldn't stand to go another moment without knowing how you really felt about me. I was so scared that I'd get here and not know what to say, or that you'd turn me down." His gaze heated, and his lips quirked into a knowing smile. "That kiss says that maybe I didn't need to worry so much."

The chemistry they shared was intoxicating, apparently even debilitating since she couldn't see or think straight around him, but it wasn't enough to erase what she'd seen behind the door of Studio Seven. Did he swoop in to make Rusty's cake and get some action before heading back to his life in L.A.? Surely he didn't think she was willing to be a stop on his Valentine's Day tour. She wasn't exactly resisting him, though. Carly straightened her spine and recovered her wits. If anyone had seen them, her hard-earned professional reputation would be compromised. Now more than ever, she should protect it, not risk it for a make-out session with the guy who'd broken her heart. No matter that nobody had ever kissed her like that before, or that nobody else made her forget everything with a single glance.

"So, you came here to make the cake and steal some kisses?" She sounded uptight to her own ears, but it was better than melting at the sight of someone who could leave her for the chance at a job and a hot blonde.

He laughed, eyes dancing with amusement. "You'll never change, will you, cupcake?" He shook his head and took her hands in his. "I came back to get you, to tell you that I've fallen for you.

I can't stand being away from you, and all I can hope is that you feel even a little bit of that."

A little bit of that? Sure, she felt a little bit of that, if he meant that she couldn't breathe from the grief of losing him, that everything changed, for the worse, when he left. Her world had flattened, the air simply gone out of it. Without Michael, everything was gray, bland, and hopeless.

"I do," she managed to squeak out past the lump forming in her throat.

"I told myself that it wasn't real, what we had. That you would've asked me to stay if you felt the same way, but I know that was a cop-out. I hoped that once a little time passed, I'd be normal again, that I'd be able to fall asleep or wake up without aching for you. It never happened. It just got worse, the longer I went without seeing you."

"Me, too. I wanted you to stay with me, but I couldn't make you give up your dream to be with me. It was too much to ask." The last word caught in her throat, and he ran his thumb across her cheek before cupping her chin in his hand.

"I'd give up anything to be with you. I'm in love with you, Carly Piper."

He sealed his statement with a kiss, sweet and full of sincerity, and she wanted to return the sentiment, but ...

"What about the show?" Another thought chilled her: what about the blonde?

"I'm nothing without you, worthless. I want you to come back with me and be my partner, whether it's in business or on the show. If you don't want to come with me, I'll stay here. Whatever it takes."

"What? Be your partner? I can't be on a television show. I can't close my shop and move away, and you can't leave your sister."

"We don't have to move. The show is shot on location, and we don't have to live in L.A. There's no reason we can't figure this out. People love you, and they love us together. Without you, I'm boring as hell—and nobody wants to watch that. Together, we're great. We'll do the show together, start our own product line, cowrite books together, whatever you want. As long as we're together, it'll be magic. We'll be a team, and it'll be perfect. Just say yes."

"It does sound like fun, and we are great together." She nudged him with her hip, smiling as the idea took hold. They did have incredible chemistry on camera, and with Michael by her side, everything was more fun. Building a brand together would be amazing.

"Wait, what about the blonde?" she blurted.

"What blonde?" Confusion clouded his eyes for a second until understanding replaced it. "You can't mean Kaitlin, can you? How do you know about her?"

"Who is she?" Not ready to admit the truth, she pressed the issue.

"She's a model, or actress, or model-slash-actress, whatever. The network won't hire her if you agree to come on board. They want you."

"She wasn't, like, a girlfriend?"

"No, of course not. She was a potential coworker, nothing more. I've met her exactly once, and it was at work. They brought her in to test as my co-host for the show. But since it hasn't aired, again, how do you know about her?"

Given his history, and his propensity for dating gorgeous blondes, it was no wonder she'd jumped to the conclusion. She was just sorry that she hadn't trusted her instincts enough to meet with him before running away. She'd been too afraid of rejection to allow him to surprise her. What a waste of time, of potential happiness!

She stared at the floor, scuffing one toe against the marble, refusing to meet his eyes. "I saw you with her."

Michael took her by the shoulders and squeezed. "Come again?"

"I went to the studio, and when I saw you, she was there, so I left."

He laughed, quick and incredulous. "Wait, are you saying that you flew to California to see me, but then you got scared and ran away at the first opportunity?"

She bit her lip and had to laugh a little herself. She was ridiculous. "Sort of."

He pulled her into his arms. "There's nobody but you. Never could be anyone but you."

Her heart sang when he pressed a kiss to the top of her head and relaxed against her. How had she doubted this? Nothing had ever felt more right. "I'm so glad you came back. I hated it without you."

"I hated it, too." He smoothed a lock of hair behind her ear and held her face in his hands, looking deeply into her eyes. "I love your heart and your mind, everything about you. When we're together, I feel like a better version of myself. Nobody makes me feel like you do, ever."

"It's like it's meant to be." She was grinning like a fool, but she couldn't stop. Didn't want to.

"It is. When you're gone, I'm not myself. You make me real. We belong together, Carly, I'm sure of it."

"You're right. We do." Sure, it could be scary but it was also absolutely the right decision. "Let's do it then. The show, the books, the works. I'm all in."

"Yeah?" Michael's grin lit up his face.

When she nodded, he scooped her into a bear hug, lifting her feet off the floor. With a sweet kiss to her forehead, he set her down and ran his fingers across her jaw. "It's going to be amazing. Let's celebrate after we finish our first job together."

Hand in hand, they returned to the reception—to celebrate the couple that had inadvertently brought them together not once, but twice—and Carly knew she'd found the man she belonged with.

Epilogue

Carly placed the final sugar rose on the Eiffel Tower cake they'd prepared for the segment and faced the camera. The cameraman counted down from five and pointed to her. "Welcome back to *Around the World in Thirteen Cakes* with Michael and Carly. We hope you enjoyed joining us on our trip to Paris, and that maybe you'll try to recreate this cake at home. We're so sad to say good-bye, not only to this beautiful city, but also to our amazing viewers, until next season. We've had a wonderful time and couldn't have done it without your support."

Things had moved at lightning speed once she signed on to join Michael on the show. They'd begun shooting immediately, before the season was even completely planned. Layla had taken over the bulk of the daily work at Caketopia, freeing Carly up to travel. They'd visited Las Vegas, New York City, Miami, and Lake Tahoe before taking the show to Toronto and Niagara Falls. Between stops, they created web content, worked on their first joint cookbook, and brainstormed ideas for a product line. It was a wonder they had time for romance, but Michael made sure they did.

"We'll be back next season, when we'll bring the fun to America's best small towns. Be sure to submit your town for consideration on our website. You never know, we might pay you a visit." Michael put his arm around Carly's shoulder. "In the meantime, be sure to check out the macaron recipe that Carly posted and let us know how yours turn out. I'd rather buy mine in a Parisian bakery, but lucky for you, Carly has enough patience to work out the perfect recipe."

Carly looked out at the beautiful city, thrilled and awed that they'd come so far. Besides being head over heels in love with

Michael, she was profoundly grateful to him. Grateful for the confidence he inspired in her, and grateful for the partner he'd become. She never would've imagined they'd end up working together side by side, building a brand and a business together. Throw in a love so complete some days she couldn't believe it was real? Bliss.

"Before we sign off, there's one more thing I need to do." Michael tapped his chest gently, his signal to Jenny that they were thinking of her while they were on the road. When they weren't in town, Michael called her every day, and Carly had come to look forward to the connection as well.

Michael cleared his throat and dropped to one knee as a production assistant wheeled the table holding their cake to the side of the makeshift set. The cameraman smiled as he focused the lens on them, clearly ready for the moment. "Carly, you are everything to me, and everything is more fun when you're there. You're my partner, my friend, the love of my life, and today I hope you'll agree to become my wife. Carly Piper, will you marry me?" He produced a velvet box from his pocket and opened it, revealing a sparkling diamond ring.

As she nodded, tears running down her cheeks, Michael placed the ring on her finger and stood. "Come here," she whispered before his lips met hers in a kiss. "Of course I'll marry you."

More from This Author
(From *A Sweet Deal* by Monica Tillery)

Richard slipped into the conference room and raised his eyebrows at his father, who waved at him to keep quiet and take a seat. One more meeting and he'd be out of the office until after the big Confectioners Association conference. Throaty laughter floated through the speaker, catching his attention and making him wonder who was on the line.

"Have you reviewed the offer? You should've received the most current information last week."

His father sat forward on his elbows and spoke into the phone. "Yes, ma'am. I've been going over the details, but I still need to meet with my son. I want him to have a clear view of what's on the table before we make any big decisions. He's going to be the one taking over when I retire." His father leaned back in his chair, a mischievous twinkle in his eye. "Of course, if he won't agree, maybe I'll just say yes so we get to spend more time together." He grinned at Richard, clearly pleased with his little joke, which only managed to set his son's teeth on edge.

"Michael, you are too much." A sexy, feminine voice wound through the conference room, smooth as melted cocoa butter and twice as decadent. "You've got to let me buy you a drink in Vegas so we can hash this out. I know you'll see things my way."

"I'd love that, Yvette, but I'm buying. I insist."

Yvette? It must be Yvette Cruz, the mergers and acquisitions representative from Saffron Sweets. The one who'd been approaching his father from every angle to convince him to agree to a buyout.

More than thirty years ago, Michael Morgan had started the family business at the urging of Richard's mother, Amelia, a fabulous cook with an unquenchable sweet tooth. The neighborhood candy shop in a quiet section of Philadelphia was an immediate success, and Richard and his brother Robert grew up amid its gleaming confectionary jars, sweeping and dusting, manning the cash register, and serving customers. They'd even assisted their mother with recipes for new confections.

The business grew rapidly during the past three decades from a thriving regional brand to a national conglomerate—all the while remaining family owned and privately held. Newer, bigger divisions arose that supplied beverages, pet care products, and household chemicals to consumers, and now Morgan Enterprises was one of the largest privately-held companies in the country with divisions spread across America.

However, with the new directions, confections had faltered and consistently lost money over the last several quarters. Selling it to Saffron Sweets, a startup chocolatier that had traded artisanship for mass-production and reaped considerable profits and growth over the last few years, made good business sense.

His father was relaxed, with a fond smile on his face, and a playful tone that matched hers in his voice. This woman represented the death of the one thing in the world Richard cared about, and his father was practically flirting with her.

"Wonderful. See you there." He could hear the smile in her voice, and it pushed his blood pressure up a few notches.

"Yep, see you soon."

They ended the call, and Richard stalked around the room, pausing to pour ice water into a crystal tumbler. He tamped down his rising irritation, unclenched his fists, and sat back down in his chair. "You already know that I don't want any division of Morgan Enterprises going public, and that includes confections. I wish you would just turn them down already. If Saffron wants to expand their product lines beyond chocolates, I don't see why they can't do that without us. I know it's not up to me, but I think this is a mistake."

He looked across the conference table at his father, who had become his mentor, his friend, and his confidante. Recently, however, they hadn't been seeing eye to eye.

"Son, I love your devotion to the company. Always have. Why you're so protective of the confections division in particular is beyond me, however. That division's been a loss leader for years, and as you know, I've been considering narrowing our focus so that pet care and chemicals gets more attention. I wouldn't mind having confections out of the picture so we can grow in other areas. Just think of how much more we could do with the profitable divisions if we shed the dead weight. It's actually lucky that they're so interested. If we sell, we can at least recoup some of our investment instead of letting confections die a slow and unprofitable death."

It never failed to surprise Richard how different their viewpoints could be despite the stubborn streak they shared. For years, that combination had kept things strained. His father had done his best, had raised Richard and his younger brother Robert with love and devotion after their mother's death, but he was busy building the business and finding the next Mrs. Morgan. He was a good father, but it wasn't until Richard was himself an adult and working with Michael in the executive offices to steer the business that they'd managed to grow closer.

"How can you say that? Candy is what made Morgan a household name! It's what we're known for, what we've always been known for. I know it isn't as lucrative as the other branches, but as a Morgan, it feels like a part of me. A part of *us*." The candy store had been his first job and his first love. For years after Amelia had passed away, Richard would visit that flagship store, convinced he could still smell her lavender perfume in the bustling kitchen.

Morgan Confectioners was a national brand, its products carried in mass retailers now, and the little Philly candy shop was long gone. Where his father saw dollars and nonexistent profit margins, Richard saw the company born from his mother's vision and hard work. Afternoons spent helping at the shop with his brother, and the time spent working as a family they'd never have again. Memories were all he had left, and he couldn't let it go without a fight. Replacing the Morgan label with Saffron's was unthinkable.

His father shook his head. "We've been over this a hundred times. Industry is about more than sentiment, son, and after I'm gone … well, you're the last Morgan in the business. I want to know that every aspect of the company is as strong as it can be. That could mean letting this one piece go for the good of the whole. I'm not sure we'll get a better offer than Saffron's, and I'd hate to see you forced into a less beneficial deal one or two years down the line."

"Dad, I'm never going to sell. I'll run everything myself once you step down in a few years. But you're still going strong, and I'm hardly the last Morgan. I'm sure Robert would come through in a crisis." He resisted the childish urge to cross his fingers on that last part. Richard's younger brother headed up his own incredibly successful record label and had no intention of ever joining the family business.

"I'm not talking about retirement; I'm talking long term here, son—our legacy," he said. "And you're the only Morgan I consider when making decisions about the company. Robert has made it very clear that he's not interested in being involved."

Richard tapped his fingers on the table and furrowed his brow. Single with no children, he could only promise to keep the company in the family as long as he lived—that much was true. They would eventually have to face the fact that Morgan could only be a family-run company as long as there were family members alive who were willing to run it.

"Richard, I know you don't want to hear this, but if you're determined to keep the business in the family, there is one other chance. It's no guarantee but it's still the best bet we've got, and I need you to consider it."

At a loss, Richard stared at his father expectantly. He'd try anything.

Michael paused for a beat and smiled, clearly amused with Richard's confusion. "You could get married."

Oh. Richard rolled his eyes and sighed. "Why does everything always come down to marriage with you?" His father loved the idea of marriage so much that he had taken the plunge two more times since the death of his beloved wife. Richard wasn't sure if the man was afraid of dying alone, trying to recreate the magic of his first fairy-tale relationship, or just in love with the idea of being in love. But it seemed that there was no limit to the chances Michael Morgan would take in his pursuit of wedded bliss.

"Don't laugh. I'm serious. A marriage means stability, children, more family. You might even like it." His father smiled kindly, the corners of his eyes crinkling.

"Because it worked out so well for me the first time?" Richard asked, his voice heavy with sarcasm.

His smile faded. "Just because it didn't work out once doesn't mean you should never try it again. I know that it's hard to believe now but not every woman is like Chelsea."

"Yes, well, thank God for that," Richard mumbled. He'd been divorced almost five years, but the lessons he'd learned still stung.

"I know. Don't you think it's been long enough, though? Do you really mean to tell me that you never want to get out there and try again? You can't let one bad experience ruin the rest of your life." His father would never truly accept that Richard was happy remaining unmarried—probably couldn't wrap his mind around it.

Richard blew out a sharp breath. "Believe it or not, I don't consider my life ruined just because I'm divorced. I'm perfectly happy concentrating on work right now, and that's all that really matters to me." Eager to move the focus away from marriage, he guided the conversation back to the acquisition. "And right now, I'm concerned. Saffron must be really serious about winning you over if Yvette's in the picture. I've heard they don't send her in unless it's critical."

Yvette Cruz was Saffron's nearly foolproof secret weapon when it came to acquiring divisions like his, and her involvement meant that things were spiraling out of his control. Rumor had it that she was beautiful, seductive, and incredibly persuasive, and knowing his father's penchant for gorgeous, younger women had Richard on high alert.

"Yvette has been in for a few meetings, yes, but you know, I'm very happy with the woman I'm seeing. She's a sharp businesswoman. She loves the new hard candies—especially the champagne lollipops—and it wouldn't hurt to strike a deal with them before they figure out that we've got nothing new coming down the pipe. They think we're a good fit for their brand, and we could push into the organic pet food market with the money we save cutting the dead weight of confections." He took a sip of water from the crystal tumbler sitting in front of him, ice tinkling against the sides.

"Dad, I don't think the confections division is dead weight. It's going through a slump, sure, but the champagne lollipops have increased interest in the brand. Once we develop something with similar impact, we'll be back in the black before we know it. I just need time. Selling to Saffron feels like giving up."

Morgan Confectioners had introduced their all-time bestselling product earlier in the year and posted their biggest sales in a decade, though it wasn't quite enough to justify the money they poured into the division. They were funneling money into research and development at unprecedented rates, trying to build on the momentum the champagne lollipops had started. Why his father couldn't see the unlimited potential ahead of them, refused to see how much a few more successful products could change things, boggled his mind.

"Well, if you're that opposed to Saffron, then you know what you have to do," his father said, a sly grin replacing the kindly smile. "If you're interested in my proposal—so to speak—then as soon as you're engaged, I will formally suspend talks of a merger with Saffron. Once you're legally married, I will turn over Morgan Confectioners to you."

Richard regarded his father and weighed the offer, considering his options. Excitement welled up at the thought of gaining outright control of Morgan Confectioners. The company was his passion, his one true love, and to have it so close, within his grasp, was a thrilling prospect.

Finding a woman who would agree to the marriage would be easy. Chelsea had proven that well enough. He'd married her for love, but it wasn't a full year before her true colors shone through. She'd been far more interested in the Morgan name and the money that went with it than with a loving marriage.

Richard had always depended on his ability to read people, to navigate situations by relying on his intuition. To have his marriage be little more than a deception rattled him terribly, landing a complete blow to his confidence. When it came to work, he always knew where he stood, what he wanted, but he doubted he'd ever be able to trust his judgment again when it came to romance.

Most of the events he attended for his charitable involvements or for business required dates, but that was as far as things went. Mentally flipping through the current selection of women he was seeing, Richard wondered if he'd actually be able go through with marrying any of them. He wouldn't do to someone else what Chelsea had done to him. No, he'd have to find a woman who stood to benefit as much as he would from the arrangement.

Or he could actually choose someone and attempt a real relationship. Right now, that was the last thing he was interested in. He'd finally reached the point after his divorce where the thought of spending time with a woman didn't turn his stomach, but there was no way in hell he was going to marry one. His marriage to Chelsea taught him one thing: he couldn't recreate the idyllic nuclear family of his childhood just because he wanted to. He'd have to figure something else out.

Richard pushed his chair back and stood as his father did the same. "Obviously I'll have to think about it, but I'll let you know what I decide. If you could hold off on making any moves with Saffron until after we return from Vegas, I would appreciate it. I'm sure Ms. Cruz will be at the conference, trying to sink her claws into you, but it will be near impossible for me to concentrate with this is on my mind."

His father straightened his jacket. "You should take a meeting with her. You might surprise yourself and actually like her. She's much less bloodthirsty than you seem to think. But of course I'll hold off on giving her an answer." He stood up. "I plan on enjoying the conference this year and hope you'll do the same. I haven't even looked at the events schedule since the packet landed on my desk, but we'll have to at least grab a drink together. See you in Las Vegas."

His father left, and Richard was alone in the opulent conference room. He slipped his hands in his pockets and looked out the window over the city skyline, the possibilities spreading out before him. Michael's somewhat indecent proposal would have to wait. The National Confectioners Association Conference was being held in Las Vegas this weekend, and it was the biggest, most important industry event of the year. Vegas was one of Richard's favorite cities in the world and he was looking forward to the conference even more than usual this year. With any luck, he'd make the necessary appearances and still have plenty of time to hit the casino. A little harmless gambling was just what he needed. It was good to be on top, and Richard intended to enjoy every moment of the conference.

• • •

Yvette brought the crystal flute of champagne to her lips as she shifted from one foot to the other. Her stilettos were gorgeous, absolute works of art, but they were little more than exquisite torture devices for her feet. After rushing between meetings and workshops all day, the pain was almost unbearable. Still, it would be a cold day in hell when she showed up at a conference in sensible shoes.

The elegant guests in the crowded hospitality suite laughed and chattered, as uniformed waiters served trays of elaborate appetizers and flutes of sparkling champagne. Industry events were absolutely necessary, but always such a bore. So little actually got accomplished until the conference was over and everyone was back at work, but the networking opportunities and connections one made were priceless. Yvette struggled to focus on the balding, paunchy man at her side droning on and on about how his company could help Saffron expand beyond chocolates, and why they were the perfect corporate match. She would give anything to meet someone interesting at one of these events for once, regardless of how they could help her career. Discreetly scanning the room, Yvette occasionally inserted what she hoped were appropriate sounds into the conversation and wished for a reprieve.

Her eyes settled on a vaguely familiar figure across the room. Richard Morgan swirled amber liquid in a cut crystal tumbler, looking as bored as she felt. The pictures she'd seen didn't do him justice. Images in print and online couldn't capture the sense of magnetism that surrounded him. That chiseled jawline, those striking green eyes, the way he seemed to command respect while completely at ease. She laid a gentle hand on her companion's forearm and flashed him a bright smile.

"Will you excuse me? I have somewhere I need to be." Without waiting for a reply, Yvette locked eyes with Richard and sashayed across the room as quickly as her delicate four-inch stiletto heels would allow. Now *this* could be interesting.

"Richard Morgan? Hi, I'm Yvette Cruz." She extended her hand to him and gave him her most professional smile. Good lord, he was handsome. She leaned in, close enough to smell his sophisticated fragrance, something lush and velvet, indefinable.

"I know who you are." His green eyes met hers in a steady gaze, and his expression gave nothing away. He didn't take her hand, and she let it drop to her side.

Yvette rearranged her features to hide her disappointment and paused for a beat, letting his icy reaction settle between them. She couldn't let him see that he had ruffled her. Shifting her weight to one leg, she pushed her shoulders back a bit, and dropped her chin so that she looked up at him through lowered lashes. "I'm so glad to finally meet you, though after spending so much time with your father, I feel like I know you already."

"I don't know what you mean, Ms. Cruz." His voice was low and deep, carefully controlled.

"Please, call me Yvette. No need for such formality." She laughed to break the tension and touched his arm. He flinched, almost imperceptibly, and kept his expression neutral. He was going to make her work for every word he uttered, but Yvette was never one to shy away from a challenge. Especially one this sexy.

He remained silent, so she continued. "I was hoping that we'd bump into one another here. I've been to the Morgan offices to meet with your father, but I could never quite catch up with you." His father never said yes to her proposals, but he was always glad to see her, was always welcoming and charming. Her encounters with Michael had been so pleasant that Richard's stonewall treatment blindsided her.

He took a sip of his drink and let out a short, humorless laugh. "Yes, I've seen you slinking around my father's office. You could have easily contacted my office to schedule a meeting with me, but I have a feeling that's not your style."

"What's that supposed to mean?"

"I just get the impression that you'd rather flirt with my father to get what you want than to deal with me directly. He's a sucker for a beautiful woman, but I am a bit more difficult to manipulate." He leveled her with a steely gaze. His eyes were intense, gorgeous, but filled with contempt.

"I have no idea what you're talking about. I've never flirted with your father, and that's not how I operate. Michael has always been charming and polite, but that's as far as it's ever gone. Our meetings have been strictly professional, unlike this conversation, and I resent the implication. It's not like I'm angling to become the fourth Mrs. Michael Morgan." She scoffed, a very unladylike sound, but his insinuation was unbelievable. Her instinct was to lash out, to defend her hard-won reputation and her professionalism, but Yvette took care to rein in her rising irritation, to keep her exterior controlled and cool. She wouldn't let him goad her into losing her temper. "I don't know why you'd expect me to schedule a meeting with you anyway. You've made it perfectly clear that you're not interested in the proposal. If my understanding is correct, your father is still the head of Morgan Confectioners." He took a small step back, apparently not prepared for her to call him out.

He paused for a beat before shaking his head, as though shaking off the remark. "He won't be in charge forever, Ms. Cruz, and unfortunately for you, he's taking my opinion on this matter under consideration. You're right, though. Meeting with me would be unnecessary as I have no interest in allowing Morgan Confectioners to be swallowed up by Saffron, and my answer will always be 'no' regardless of the offer. We're doing just fine on our own."

Yvette's lips formed a conciliatory smile. Morgan Confectioners was a sinking ship, and Saffron was itching to throw it a life vest. Richard was determined to deny that the other divisions were keeping it on life support, for whatever reason. She had to maintain control, show him that he couldn't rattle her with hostility. Time to kill him with kindness and professionalism, as she had a deal to broker. "Everyone would agree that Morgan Enterprises is doing fine, but your confections division is another story. You've got something we want, and I think we'd make a good team. What we're proposing would be good for everyone."

"You could dip that offer in your company's finest chocolate, and I still wouldn't bite."

He practically snarled, but she laughed. She had to admire his determination, as foolish as it seemed. "I assure you this is a sweet deal, even unembellished. We do pride ourselves on having the country's finest chocolate, though, and I'd be happy to send you some."

"Ms. Cruz," he said, adding emphasis on each syllable "I will never, under any circumstances, surrender on this issue."

"I can't decide if you sound more like a soap opera villain or a petulant child. Why can't we discuss this like adults, like professionals?"

"Because there's nothing to discuss."

"Have you even read our proposal? I'd be interested in hearing your thoughts, and I'd be happy to address any concerns you might have. At this stage, nothing is set in stone, and if there's something specific that you take issue with, I'd love to discuss it."

"No, I haven't read your proposal, and I'm not going to. I don't need to read it to know that I don't want Saffron's slick, generic mark on the products I love."

Now he went too far. Brand popularity didn't equal inferior product, and she wouldn't let Richard Morgan throw her off her game. "Saffron is known all over the country for our chocolate, and unlike Morgan, we're flourishing in a down economy." She flashed him a cool smile. "People love what we offer, and there's no reason to think we can't expect the same success with rebranded Morgan products."

"I'd rather be smaller but offer superior quality, rather than carelessly mass-producing and underpricing my competitors."

"And that's why your other divisions are outperforming confections by millions of dollars each year." She asserted sharply.

His eyebrow raised, and he sized her up with a narrowed gaze. Yvette shifted her weight, staring back and refusing to stand down as the tension strummed between them. "Touché, Ms. Cruz," he finally replied. Did the corner of his lips actually rise in a semblance of a smile or was that a trick of the low ballroom lighting?

"Listen, having wider distribution and a bigger marketing campaign doesn't mean you have to sacrifice quality. People in this country are still interested in originality and innovation. They just like buying from a brand they know, and they want it at a good price."

He frowned, considering. "You have a point, of course, but Morgan Confectioners is more to me than a revenue stream. It's a family business, something I care for very deeply."

She smiled. "I certainly understand the importance of family. I love mine, and owe everything I am to them. But didn't your father ever teach you that business and emotions don't mix?" Yvette took a chance and sidled closer, laying a hand on his arm and squeezing gently. "We love what you've developed so much that we want it for ourselves. You should be flattered," she added, her voice light and teasing. Any other man *would* be flattered. Why Richard Morgan was immune to her attention was a mystery.

He closed the distance between them and leaned down so that his lips almost touched her ear. His breath was hot against her skin and sent goose bumps erupting down her arms. He was close enough to kiss, and her breath caught in her throat as she waited to see what he would do.

"No. Deal." His firm words shouldn't have been arousing, but it was all she could do to resist the urge to find out what his mouth would feel like crushed against hers.

"Richard, this is the best offer you're likely to get. You should really give it some thought before you dismiss it." The sad truth was that if Saffron didn't buy them out, the confections division would continue to suck money from the rest of Morgan Enterprises until they found a way to turn it around.

"I've heard enough."

Yvette felt oddly disappointed by the finality of his words. Her lips wanted to find their way to his, to change his mind about *her*, if not the deal itself, but he turned and walked away.

Watching his broad back as he disappeared into the crowd, Yvette enjoyed the view despite herself. He would come around; they always did. Yvette Cruz didn't back down from a fight.

She'd come from nothing and had worked her whole life to get to where she was at Saffron Sweets. Everything she had, she had earned, and none of it had come easy what with her past. Nobody had given her a thing in life, ever, except for her parents, who had worked too hard for her to let a little setback like Richard Morgan stop her. Not after what she'd been through in her lifetime. Her hand fluttered subconsciously to her chest, her fingers tracing the ridged skin concealed by the high neckline of her dress.

To have her work belittled so casually, so flippantly, was infuriating. Almost as infuriating as her burning attraction to this man. She refused to accept that this would be their only encounter, and in truth, she couldn't wait to see what the next meeting would hold. After all, she always enjoyed a challenge.

Across the room, Richard approached a pretty brunette and stopped to chat. The other woman looked up at him with wide, adoring eyes, and as he smiled, laughed, and touched her arm, Yvette finally turned away. She finished her champagne with three long sips, set the empty glass on the nearest table, and strode toward the exit with her shoulders back and her head held high. As she passed Richard, she threw him a mental salute: *Till we meet again.*

• • •

Richard took a slow swallow of his single malt scotch, winced as it burned a trail down his throat, and watched Yvette glide out of the hospitality suite. What an aggravating temptation she was. Her cool, unflappable calm in the face of his disdain had just inflamed his desire more. Nobody stood up to him like that, ever, and part of him was eager to see what giving in to her would feel like—much to his dismay. The young food sciences chemist at his side was chattering excitedly about those effervescent lollipops she had developed for the company, and he knew he should give her his full attention, but his mind was on Yvette. Her obvious agenda irritated him, but her lush curves and impressively quick wit lingered in his mind, making it hard for him to remember why he'd wanted her gone. Beautiful women were easy to come by, but one with brains to match was a rare find, and one of his few weaknesses.

Richard was glad she'd left when she did though, as he'd been dangerously close to finding out if her lips were as soft and lush as they looked. He imagined they would be warm, and sweet with the champagne she'd been drinking. The thought gave rise to an unwelcome stirring deep within his body. What was wrong with him? The woman was after his company, and he had to remember that if he had any hope of protecting it. Focusing on the young brunette standing before him, he forced his mind off Yvette and her delicious curves. Or tried to.

" … I mean, I was nervous at first, but the session went really well. I think everyone enjoyed it. I mean, they paid attention and asked a lot of questions when I finished." The young woman paused, apparently waiting for his response, and he snapped back to attention. She was filling him in on the discussion panel she had run that afternoon as a representative of their company, and she was obviously looking for praise.

He smiled down at her, turning on his signature charm. "I'm sure they did. Everybody wants something like your lollipops for their company. It's nice that you could provide some insight and maybe inspiration, but I'm certainly glad that Morgan Confectioners is the one that has you."

"You're so sweet to say so, Mr. Morgan. I'm glad to be a part of the company, and I hope to stay on after the buyout. I know that a lot of things change in these situations, but we're all praying that the department gets by relatively unscathed." She took a sip of her drink and watched him expectantly.

"Buyout? Rebecca," he watched her face to see if he got her name right, "there will be no buyout. Morgan has always been family owned, and we have no intention of changing that."

Her cheeks flushed, and her eyes darted around the room. "Oh, Mr. Morgan, I apologize. I suppose we've all heard the Saffron rumors and have obviously made more of it than was necessary. I shouldn't have said anything."

Richard relaxed his grip when he realized he was squeezing his glass almost hard enough to crack it. He hadn't expected news of his father's talks with Saffron to get out so quickly when so few people knew about them. Still, it was important for him to know what misinformation was circling, and he couldn't let his irritation show. "Saffron is looking to expand their product line beyond chocolate, and they've expressed interest in buying our confections division. But I've let them know in no uncertain terms that we're not interested. Anything you've heard is nothing more than conjecture. You've nothing to worry about."

Rebecca looked like she wanted to say more, but she sipped her champagne and remained silent. She shifted from one foot to the other, looking increasingly agitated, and Richard excused himself. He had obviously made her uncomfortable, and he was too distracted to make polite conversation with an employee. The scientist's relief was noticeable as he told her to enjoy the evening and wished her goodnight.

Richard finished his scotch in one burning swallow and set the empty tumbler on a table as he strode towards the door, anxious to get out of the room. He didn't know where he was headed, but it would be easier to think if he escaped the claustrophobic atmosphere of the crowded party. Yvette had invaded his business life and now had somehow managed to wind her way into his personal life, driving him to maddening distraction. She was beautiful—exquisite even—but he wasn't exactly inexperienced when it came to exceptional women. He never let personal matters interfere with his professional obligations. What was so different about her and how could he get her out of his system?

When she was just a name and face he'd glimpsed only briefly, he'd had a semblance of control. Now she was a three-dimensional threat to his sanity, and Richard needed to do something—anything—to push her off his radar. That would be nearly impossible when all he could think about was how soft her skin must be, how sweet her lips would taste beneath his.

He stormed out of the hospitality suite and punched the elevator button with much more force than necessary. Cursing both the wait and his uncharacteristic impatience, he pressed the button again.

"Will that make the elevator arrive faster?" The sultry voice matched the intoxicating fragrance invading his space and wound its way through his body.

So much for control.

"A delightful novella romance. Tales of music stars finding love will adore Tillery's first book and will sigh with a smile at the end."—*In D'Tale Magazine*

"*Kiss Me, Katie* is a heartwarming love story with the music scene at its core. Strong, well-developed characters along with a great plot makes you feel like you're in the audience at one of their sold-out concerts. Sit back and enjoy the show. You'll be glad you did!"—Romance Junkies

In the mood for more Crimson Romance?
Check out by *Winning Streak* at *CrimsonRomance.com*.